MW01138149

Carol Maupin

authorHOUSE®

AuthorHouse™
1663 Liberty Drive
Bloomington, IN 47403
www.authorhouse.com
Phone: 1 (800) 839-8640

Published by AuthorHouse 10/05/2017

ISBN: 978-1-5462-0882-2 (sc)
ISBN: 978-1-5462-0880-8 (hc)
ISBN: 978-1-5462-0881-5 (e)

Library of Congress Control Number: 2017914382

Print information available on the last page.

Any people depicted in stock imagery provided by Thinkstock are models, and such images are being used for illustrative purposes only. Certain stock imagery © Thinkstock.

This book is printed on acid-free paper.

Because of the dynamic nature of the Internet, any web addresses or links contained in this book may have changed since publication and may no longer be valid. The views expressed in this work are solely those of the author and do not necessarily reflect the views of the publisher, and the publisher hereby disclaims any responsibility for them.

CONTRIBUTORS PAGE

I would like to thank those who helped me put this book together. Casey Vogt and Andrew Campbell. Thank you for all your hard work. To all my friends who believed in me no matter what and encouraged me to keep writing. Thank you Cassandra Barker for my author photo.

DEDICATION PAGE

I would like to dedicate Revenge in the Bluegrass to my mother Shirley Ann who was my hero in life.

To my Father Bernard Wayne and Stepmother Betty for raising me to do what's right.

CHAPTER 1

*M*attie knew her life would never be the same, for the object in her possession was powerful. This news would affect the everyday people in the small rural Kentucky town of Beaver Dam. Her hands trembling from the weight of the object, her heart raced as endless thoughts flooded her mind, with sweat dropping of the crook of her nose. The only thing keeping her grounded in this situation was gravity, but the gravity of this current situation would drive a normal person mad with fear. Her body shot up with a burst of adrenaline, as she tried to come to terms with the events prior to this day.

"Alright, get a grip," she thought, "It's time."

The object she held in her hands was getting heavier and heavier with each passing minute. Mattie wanted to be free from this nightmare. She ran to the nearest mailbox, opened the lid, and dropped an envelope with contents that could save her life and clear her of any unforeseeable happenings. The envelope would now be in the hands of the Attorney General, Jax McCarthy.

Attorney McCarthy was handsome with dark wavy hair coiffed, piercing blue eyes, and a smile that could win an argument in a courtroom. He was admired by his fellow peers, earning the respect of the Kentucky Democratic Party. Some of his finest accolades include receiving the most votes within his political position, earning him the nickname as the "Democrat's Golden Boy," something he knew fondly. Politics ran in the family, his grandfather was one of the most beloved Governors of the Commonwealth, something was also in his favor. Most likely if the elections were held at that very moment, his chances of winning were null and void, especially after the last year he had. "Hope springs eternal," he thought. Jax was a good man with a big heart, something rare for someone in his position to have. Kentucky lawyers were supposed to be heartless sharks with a flair for dramatics in the courtroom. He was that, but in his heart, was the burning for the challenge.

And the most prized of fights, was the one for Kentucky. In his earlier days, he was tough, the fighter of justice, unknowingly Kentucky's Knight in shining armor.

Mattie McGraw, the baby of her family, grew up in the small coal-mining town of Beaver Dam. Mattie was the fragile child born into the world fighting, weighing only three pounds at birth. She was fascinated by the world around her, curious and eager to learn more, something that often got her in trouble. Little did she know her world would turn upside down with her trust evaporating. Because of her steadfast curiosity, she would quickly learn about the enemies who would want to take her life and wreck it into pieces. My husband is dead. They've taken my child away from me. I have nothing left to lose. It was pouring rain in Lexington all day long, sending people away from their homes to shelters. Lexington was hit hard by pellets of rain flooding streets, homes and moving cars. Some unfortunately, with their unhappy owners still in them. According to the news this was the worst rain that had hit in one hundred years and no one was quite ready for it. Mattie had lived in Lexington for about seven years, it had become her home, but unfortunately, she had to keep moving to stay alive.

Mattie had been driving for hours around the city getting on and off New Circle Road taking her around the city with no known destination. She was afraid for her life and the trembling wouldn't stop. Finally, she decided to find a place to stay outside the city. It was a rundown motel called the Lucky Seven. Although at this time she wasn't feeling too lucky. She checked in under the name Tabatha Smith. She knew she couldn't use her credit cards, too risky.

She had sixty dollars to her name, enough to stay for a couple of nights and carefully figure out what her next moves would be. She ascended the creaky stairs, slowly reaches for the doorknob and opened the door to her temporary haven. The room itself was depressing, smelling of a stale smoke that lingered. She threw her overnight bag down on the floor, and lunged into the bed, oblivious to the stained yellowed walls and the two dead cockroaches that laid lifeless. She knew the place was a dump, but couldn't care less.

The next morning came as she anticipated. "I'm alive, I'm breathing," she thought. She was exhausted from the endless nightmares that plagued her thoughts. She restlessly tossed and turned all throughout the night hoping to wake up from this "dream" she was having. Sadly, this was her new reality. Her husband Ben dead and her daughter Melina was still missing. "Everything is going to Hell all around me," she thought, "but at least I'm alive and that's all that matters for now." She was at ease knowing the contents of that envelope would soon be in Jax McCarthy's hands. Jax was an honest, trustworthy man, unlike the Governor. Jax would be the hero against that monster who killed Ben, her better half, her compassionate, spontaneous husband. As she began reflecting on her deceased husband the memories of the life they created together began pouring in, two wonderstruck years that they spent creating a family. Some say opposites attract, in this case there was a great truth to that. For Mattie was the serious, responsible one while Ben acted as the comedian, the prankster who would call his in-laws on April Fool's Day or pull pranks that would leave him laughing for days. They both shared a mutual love for Motown music, and Mattie was charmed by how Ben could dance one hell of a mamba.

The two had met during their college years at Western Kentucky University where Ben received a full ride baseball scholarship and had met at a fraternity party in the first week. Mattie knew he was the one from that first encounter for she was swayed by the gorgeous locks of red hair and the dreamy blue eyes that glistened brighter when he smiled back at her. From across the room the two made eye contact when Mattie decided to take matters into her own hands by making the first move.

There was something to be said about the way Ben gazed into her eyes that night. Maybe it was the way she could light up a room with her personality, or maybe it was the alcohol talking, but all he could think of was how she smiled and how he wouldn't stop thinking of her after that night. He thought maybe I'll marry that girl and we'll be together forever. Unfortunately, somethings never come to fruition.

CHAPTER 2

*I*t was a normal day at the office for Jake Estevan, Private Investigator. The women back in Beaver Dam loved Jake, often fantasizing him as their ideal man for a one-night stand. Jake was a tall man with an athletic build. Blessed with jet-black wavy hair from his mother's Hispanic heritage, he also wore silky loose-fitting pants that couldn't hide his shapely musculature form.

One thing that can be said about Jake is that he too loved the women of Beaver Dam, going through them like freshly baked chocolate chip cookies. He was never fully satisfied with just one woman, going from one affair to another, he often thought about that one woman who got away from the small town to pursue bigger and grander things. Jake knew from the first time he laid eyes on Madeline *"Mattie"* McGraw that she was the perfect woman for him. Mattie in those days wasn't the prettiest girl in her high school years, but there was something about her in her unconventional beauty. She wasn't like the other babes who dressed like drive-in sluts and just went out for a good slam.

Mattie was sophisticated and classy, upright as if she were royalty on authority from the Queen herself. At Beaver Dam High, there were two main social groups: The Have's and the Have-Not's. The former comprised of super jocks and athletic preppies while the latter were poor kids having very little to their name, but they knew how to have a good time on a Saturday night. Jake found himself intrigued by the Have-Not's.

Jake could recall the day he first met Mattie. It was during a scorching August day where the tempers were also hot. That day a fight broke out between Antonio Scollini, a brute and Lil' J who was loved as most popular at Ohio County High. Scollini was furious over the rumors that Lil' J was sleeping with his girlfriend Rhonda. Scollini swings a punch, "you bastard, I'm going to kick your puny ass," he screamed. Rhonda was loving every moment of it. She was considerably the most popular girl in high school, blessed from a gene pool of a great body, platinum blonde hair that rested atop her head, and a smile that could make a man weak. She was the epitome of every high schooler's dream.

Scollini's fist made impact with Lil' J's face when he least expected it. The dirty fighter hit with such force that Lil' J fell to the concrete floor with one swing. "Get up, you loser," taunted Scollini. But in that moment, the crowd knew the fight was over. With Lil' J knocked out unconscious, Scollini was far from done with his revenge. Hovering over the comatose body, Scollini continued taunting, "get up damn it and fight like man." His rage only drove him to take more evasive measures. Scollini reached for something out of his pocket, wielding a sharpened switch blade. Mattie caught sight of the blade and was determined to save Lil' J when he couldn't defend himself. "Enough already," screamed Mattie, "you've already won, get that away from his throat." A devious smile appeared on Scollini's face, he never used the blade on a girl before, but in his tormented mind the curiosity piqued his interests.

Scollini was a thug, born into a family of crime and violence. His father was incarcerated for beating his first wife, nearly killing her. Fighting was all that Antonio Scollini knew. His father would come home drunk every night and destroying everything in sight. Sometimes it was dinner flung on the wall, or punching a different family member just for fun. Antonio knew how to be quiet in these situations, no movements or sounds, sometimes no breathing. Anything and everything would set his father's temper off.

Every night Antonio was tormented by the screams of his mother, but after a while he learned to block out the noises and go about his nights. "Maybe she had it coming," he thought, "maybe she deserved to be hit." No one was around to explain to him that hitting was wrong. Antonio liked the power that surged from people fearing him. In a way, he too would become more like his father each day. Mattie was the only person brave enough to see past this powerful brute. She reached for his forearm trying to knock the blade from his hands. Scollini struggled to take back control. Jake hearing the altercation, saw the heroic gesture Mattie was making. He pushed past other people to save her from making a regrettable mistake. Jake reaches into the center, grabs Mattie by the shoulders, tripping backwards with Mattie landing on top of him. In that moment, their eyes locked onto each other, a grin appeared on Jake's face as if he were a cat that just captured a canary. Mattie wanted to meet Jake desperately, but she hadn't pictured it this way. "Get away from me," she cried. He backed off slowly with his hands up in the air. Before anything else could happen, the principal broke up the main fight taking Scollini for disciplining while an ambulance took away Lil' J swiftly. It was learned that Lil' J suffered from a concussion with three broken ribs.

Mattie was handed a handkerchief for the blood dripping down her nose. Enamored by her piercing green eyes, Jake thought still she was hot even with the bloody mess on her face. He liked a challenge, especially a girl who never backed down from a fight. "I'm sorry I stepped in..," Jake retorted, "it's just I thought you were about to take a huge beating back there." "I'm fine, perfectly capable of taking care of myself," she replied. "It's just Scollini is a bully, he'll hit anyone or anything that moves," he replied. "A bully is only that until you stand up to them." Jake admired her blaring confidence and her candor.

"Maybe we should get that bloody nose of yours checked out, it might be broken after all. I mean." "Again, don't worry about me, I'll be fine," she assured him. She was cajoled by Scollini, detesting him by the way he threatened everyone with his presence. Jake on the other hand had her full and undivided attention being wooed by his charm.

"By the way, name's Jake," he mentioned. "I know who you are, I've seen you in the halls. Your reputation precedes you," she replied. Jake taunted, "don't believe everything that you always hear...at least what the girls say about me." "Oh wow, I'm in the presence of a legend and I never knew it." His charm and smile made her weak kneed, as if the earth itself moved when he spoke to her.

Mattie wasn't concerned about his reputation, she wanted to be with him regardless. In the back of her mind she knew that good girls never went for Jake Estevan and there was an unknown reason for it. This yearning desire to find out pushed Mattie to discover what made him tick. After spending most of high school doing the same stay-at-home routine, she was finally going to go out with him and throw caution to the wind. For once, she wanted to be a bad girl.

CHAPTER 3

$\mathcal{M}$attie tossed and turned in the dank motel room, hallucinating sounds from her daughter Melina. She yearned to be reunited and hold her sweet little girl once more. Never has she been this long without her daughter, her miracle child so to speak. Mattie had a rough time growing up, discovering from an early age that she was diagnosed with Turner's Syndrome. This condition as the doctor explained stunted her growth and incapacitated her chances of becoming a mother. Mattie learned later in life that doctors don't always have the answers and that the fact miracles can happen. Eight months ago, she gave birth to a happy, healthy little girl. The events of yesterday came stumbling forward. A rush of tears came pouring down her face like an icy waterfall.

Tiny little drops, one after another as her body shook uncontrollably, rocking back and forth. The only comfort she had was Melina's plush white teddy bear that screamed "Momma" over and over whenever she gripped the bear too tightly. She thought to herself, "Why is he tormenting me? Who killed Ben? Where is Melina and how will I ever get her back?" These questions came flooding through her tired, overworked brain. She took a deep breath and exhaled slowly. "I can't do this alone anymore, I need help." She reached for the phone next to her on the nightstand. It was time that she brought in the only man that could protect Mattie once more. The only man that could find her daughter, and get justice for Ben. It was time for her to have a chat with Jake Estevan.

It was a slow workday in the Private Investigator's office. No jealous wives calling to track down their lying, cheating husbands or no missing persons to report. Nobody called him except for that one call from the telephone company informing about the final warning on his phone bill. This news was delivered from the company's customer representative Mary. Jake hated lying to that sweet, elderly woman on the other end of the phone telling her that the bill would be resolved by the end of the week. Jake was full of crap, and he knew this. He often daydreamed in that small office of his, fantasizing that a tall, blonde Marilyn Monroe damsel in distress would come walking through those doors. These were the moments he looked forward to. Things were often slow in Beaver Dam, and the money flow problem was cramping Jake's lifestyle.

Jake grew accustomed to a certain way of living. Only the best from Giorgio Armani draped over his sleek, sexy statuesque body. Only the most beautiful of women draped in his arms, usually lonely rich widows who sought comfort in the arms of man candy. He earned the nickname *Mr. Noncommittal*. Sure, the sex was great, but that was getting old. Jake was looking for some real action.

As he started dozing off, the phone rang. He thought nothing of it. The phone rang a second and third time as he thought it was bill collectors again. Ignoring the phone was something he was good at, especially if it had anything to do with bill collectors. He let the machine pick up the phone call as his dreams were more important to him.

A panicked, but familiar voice spoke, *"Jake, Jake..it's Mattie McGraw. Please pick up the phone. I need you."" This is important. I'm not sure what to do, I'm scared, absolutely scared."* Before she could say another word, he quickly reached for the phone answering her pleas. "Mattie, how in the world are you? What it's been 10 years since high school?" "Jake, I don't have time for small talk. I need you, badly." "Where are you and are you okay," he replied. "All I can say is I'm outside of Lexington at an old rundown motel called *The Lucky Seven*." "I'm quite familiar with that place, but stay right where you are and don't do anything til I get there." "Please hurry," she screamed. Maybe it was the way her voice sounded that he knew she was truly in trouble. Jake could sense the tenseness of the situation. Mattie's voice was breathy and nervous. His body shot up out of his chair like a torpedo. He grabbed his armani jacket, and ran so fast he nearly fell down the stairs to get to his car.

"Mattie McGraw calling me after all this time, he thought. Out of all the people Jake worked for through the years, he never expected to see Mattie McGraw again or hear from her. Mattie meant everything to Jake in high school and then she left. It didn't matter Mattie needed him now. Now was all that mattered. He hoped he would get there in time to save her from whoever was chasing her.

Jake would move heaven and earth to get near her. He cursed at the car trying to kick over the engine. "Go damn it, work already!" The car couldn't have moved fast enough as far as he was concerned. Forty-five minutes passed, riding on bumpers and cutting off enraged drivers, Jake was close to reaching Lexington. He was concerned about her safety, but he knew Mattie wasn't the kind of girl to go looking for trouble. As he remembered, she was solid and stable, being grounded and humbled. These were the things he loved about her. Whatever the trouble, he was there like old times to save her, almost as if she never went away.

Jake let his guns do the talking, especially when facing unreasonable clients, it seemed to work every time. Whatever trouble it was, Jake hoped he would get there in time. He put his foot on the gas and exceeded the speed limit by 80 mph.

Mattie was restless as she tried sitting in the dark, lonely motel room. She had a feeling that Jake would come to her aid, but she knew she couldn't afford any risks of getting others involved. She was on a deadline, and her life was on the line. She felt uneasy and knew if Jake didn't get to Lexington before they found her, it would all be over.

She peeked out the blinds of the window slowly as she saw the nighttime sky settling in. She noticed an oncoming car pulling up into the parking lot. She recognized that face, that saving grace that was Jake. Without hesitation, she darted out the door to meet him coming at him with a swoop. There Jake embraced her with opened arms as if meeting an old friend again. Her heart was beating profusely at the sight of him. While gazing at him, she missed the car pulling up on the side. Suddenly, sounds of loud, screeching tires escalated from a distance. She turned in the direction of the noises and darted away. Nothing about that moment seemed real, everything felt like a motion picture with the screeching tires, the headlights and the feeling of all this in slow motion. Mattie again darted out of the way when Jake once again grabbed her like before and pushed her aside. He was ready, pulling out his .38 shooting at the black buick as it sped off. "Are you ok?" "I am now that you're here." "Let's get out of here before they come back." Jake and Mattie jumped into his 1962 Thunderbird and took off into the night. "This is the second time you've come to my rescue." Jake was speechless, he couldn't take his eyes off Mattie. "Ummmm, Darlin' you're welcome!" "So what kind of trouble are you in?"

"Who's after you," asked Jake curiously.

Mattie had to get a load off her chest and needed a stiff drink to ease her troubled mind. She suggested a drive-thru liquor store, preferably a Maker's Mark.

CHAPTER 4

They drove to the other end of Lexington to a mom and pop liquor store. They purchased two cokes and a bottle of Maker's Mark. Jake reached into the glove compartment bypassing all the unpaid parking tickets grabbing two paper cups. They ended up in old school yard that was abandoned and seemed safe to both. Jake mixed the drinks and handed one to Mattie who seemed very frayed. She slowly lifted the cup and inhaled the drink letting it drip down her full red lips.

Normally, this would have been Jake's first move with one of his babes, but this wasn't the time or the place. Jake turned off the engine and the lights. It was very, very quiet except the crickets chirping all around them. He looked at Mattie seriously. "What's going on Mattie?" "Whose after you?" "I don't know where to start." She slowly placed the cup on her lap and took a deep, deep breath.

"Just start from the beginning, try not to leave out any details, ok?" She smiled at him. "I've been working for the Governor as his secretary and assistant for the past three years. "Monday started out like any normal day." "I got up and made breakfast for Ben and Melina, my husband and daughter." "I kissed them goodbye and went to work." She placed her hand on her forehead trying to remain calm, but her hands were shaking.

"I didn't know I would be kissing Ben goodbye for the last time." Tears rolled down her red cheeks, she was mourning her dead husband. "I arrived at work just like I do every day." "The Governor was in and out the whole day in meetings." "So, everything was

12

normal." "Yeah, I guess you could say that." "Well, earlier in the day he was acting a little fidgety and nervous." "He said he was expecting an important package."

"Did he mention what was in it?" "No, I didn't have a clue." "I always open all his mail and separate the important stuff to the junk mail." "He always said that he didn't have time to read everything, that was my job." "I figured it helped him out too, so I didn't mind." "A package arrived about 4:00 pm that was bulky and taped very tightly." "I started opening it and pictures came pouring out." "Who were the pictures of Mattie?"

Tears welled up in her eyes. She put her hand over her mouth and slowly took a deep breath. "The Governor's opponent." "Seth Jenkins was the Governor's nemesis." "Sam really despised him." "Seth was rising in the polls and causing quite a stir." "What's so bad about that?" "The pictures were very graphic!" "He was dead!" "How do you know he was dead?" 'He was covered in blood, motionless." "His color was blue and Seth was in a fetal position."

"There were other pictures." "Seth was with another woman and definitely not his wife." "After I looked at the pictures, the Governor walked out of his office." "I panicked Jake!" "I dropped the pictures and they went flying all over the floor." "I picked them up and frantically tried to shove them back into the envelope." 'As I was raising up, my eyes met with the Governor." "I was frozen with fear." "He knew that I saw everything." "Mattie I've been expecting a package he replied cooly, but it's obvious you've already seen it!" "No one has to know about this Mattie!" "Let's talk about it in my office."

No one else was in his office, which made her even more scared to face him. Before Mattie knew she was going to say, the words "Murderer" blurted out of her quivering mouth. Mattie shook her head. Who was this monster standing in front of me, she pondered. Mattie adored the Governor, he had been like a father to her for the past few years.

Sam was her best man at the wedding, no one cried more tears of joy for her than Sam. He was also the godfather to Melina, her miracle baby. The Governor gave Mattie a sorrowful look as if she were a child being disciplined by her father. "Mattie come into my office and I'll explain everything." "You have pictures of a dead man that was your opponent in the Governor's race." "I wouldn't believe you anyway."

Sam had a powerful presence and Mattie loved him just like a father. However, at this moment she was petrified and scared to breathe. "Mattie, you know that I can't let you leave this office with that package, my political career would be over as well as my life!" "Please, please try to understand!" Mattie wanted to believe him so badly with every bone in her body. The pictures spoke differently.

"Mattie, the Governor reached for the envelope in Mattie's shaking hands. 'You killed a man Sam, how do I reckon with that?" She had to get out of there. If he killed once, he'll kill again, she thought. Mattie was very good at instincts. It was time to go. She grabbed her purse and car keys and ran furiously with the package clung tightly underneath her arms. In the background, the Governor's voice was screaming loudly "Mattie!" "Come back here now!" Traffic was heavy coming down the freeway, but Mattie made it home in less than thirty minutes.

Her phone calls to Ben were unanswered. "Please pick up the phone Ben!" "I need you now!" Ben would know what to do, she thought. Mattie just wanted to be held by Ben and to hold her daughter Melina in her arms and to forget this volatile day ever happened. It was too late however, things were already set in motion.

Mattie pulled up to the house. The house she and Ben loved so very much. The house her and Ben spent every penny to buy and fix up. It was a real fixer upper according to the real estate agent. It was an old white Victorian house that hadn't been occupied for years. Ben hated it, he had got his first real job with one of the most prestigious law firms in Lexington and he only wanted the best for Mattie, this house was not it.

Ben had worked hard to make it through law school and was determined to spend every penny he earned while he was alive. He only wanted the best things in life.

Mattie was more frugal and the simple things seemed to make her happy. Mattie didn't care about the money. She liked challenges and this house was everything she always wanted. Also, the fact that it had a huge backyard, a garden, and a gazebo in the front of the yard didn't hurt either. Mattie was three months pregnant with Melina when they decided to purchase their first house. It was decided that Ben would work and she would spend the next six months preparing the fixer upper for their baby.

The design of the house was large, plenty of room for three. Mattie decided it just needed a woman's touch. Decorating the bottom floor was easy. She chose black and white for the living room with large geometric rugs covered the vast wooden floors with a black elegant wood table with gold rim and velvet black and beige chairs. This was fitting for a lawyer's house and dinner parties with Ben's law firm.

Mattie carefully chose the furniture for Ben's downstairs office from the wide cherry wooden desk to the antique lamps sitting on his desk. The only thing he insisted on was that this was the Kentucky room. This was important to Ben so Mattie made sure that all prints were of the Kentucky Wildcats NCAA championships.

Especially his favorite, his photograph of the wildcats slamming the winning dunk against Sarasota. Those were good times.

March madness with all the lawyers over screaming at the television for a three pointer and bellowing out in ecstasy when the job was done. Basketball meant everything to the people of Kentucky. For Ben and Mattie, it wasn't just a sport, it was a religion. Mattie intentionally saved Melina's room for last waiting on specially ordered wallpaper with baby lambs with pink bows and blue clouds. From the ceiling hung a chandelier that sparkled like diamonds.

The baby's room was finished with an antique baby cradle painted in pink and white stripes that rocked back and forth with a musical pink and blue bunny mobile that harmoniously booted out rock-a-by-baby over and over. Ben hated that song as Mattie played it every single day while she was preparing her room.

Mattie was determined for Melina to know real music and appreciate the tunes of Marvin Gaye and the Temptations ringing through the house. This baby was going to know real music with real depth and heart and soul. Motown was more fun with a lot more soul. Mattie loved her life with Melina and working on the political front in the Governor's office. She felt like what she did mattered. "Now, it's all over!" "What happened when you got to the house Mattie?"

She hesitated for a moment. It was difficult for her to talk about finding Ben and Melina gone. It was pure agony. She felt so betrayed by Sam and couldn't understand why he would do something like this. "The house was quieter than usual."

"Ben always had our music playing through the house." "No Motown, no Ben singing to Melina." "There was nothing but dead silence." "I ran in and the house was ransacked." "The house was turned upside down." "My usually neat and organized house was torn apart from top to bottom." Mattie stepped in the kitchen first. Nothing was left on the shelves. Everything was pulled off the cupboards. The dishes were scattered everywhere, broken, jagged pieces of glass all over the floor. Mattie didn't know what she was walking into, it was unrecognizable.

She began screaming for her husband as she ran throughout the house in a panic. In the living room, pictures were ripped off the wall, lamps turned over, especially one Mattie didn't see coming as she tripped over it and fell on top of Ben. "Ben was still, not moving." "I tried to wake him up." "Then I realized he had taken a bullet to the back of his head." "I don't think he knew what was coming." Mattie screamed when she saw the blood on her hands. Ben was bleeding profusely and was dead from the gunshot.

The only words she could muster were "No, no, no!" Mattie held Ben for a few minutes stroking his hair and reliving all the good memories they had together. She had to find Melina now. Ben was dead. Her wonderful, loving husband was gone.

Mattie kissed Ben's head and gently removed it from her lap. She hurriedly walked to Melina's room terrified of what was coming. God help me she thought. Let the baby be ok she prayed. The baby's room was perfect. Nothing out of place. Except for one thing, where was Melina? A cool breeze was blowing through an open window. "I stuck my head out and saw an elderly woman with a baby running to a gray Lexus."

Mattie recognized the car. She'd seen it a hundred times at the Governor's mansion. It was one of his cars. Mattie fled downstairs to grab her daughter from this stranger, but it was too late. She screamed for her to give Melina back to her, but she blew out of the driveway like a tornado. The tires were spinning leaving dust in the wind.

"When she drove off I could hear Melina crying." Mattie ran to the kitchen to call the police, but the phone rang sending Mattie's heart soaring and skipping beats. She grabbed her chest. She let it ring over and over then finally grabbing it to make the ringing stop. "Mattie is that you?" "I know you're there." He whispered. The voice sent chills down her spine. She recognized the voice. It was the Governor with a stern voice.

"Mattie, you know what I want, just give me the package!" "No one else has to get hurt." "Where's my daughter, I want her back!" "The package for your daughter, Mattie." The Governor hung up abruptly and there was dead silence. Mattie wasn't born yesterday.

Sure, she was naïve, but she wanted to live for her little girl. Mattie knew if she gave those pictures back, she was dead too. The only thing on Mattie's mind right now was sweet revenge. She loved Sam and believed in him with all her heart. Her heart was that of a small child, trusting in everyone good, even when the rumors around the office floated out so negatively. She felt sick of her stomach. The Maker's Mark didn't agree with her. "That's when I left." "I knew if I stayed, I'd be." Mattie couldn't finish the sentence. Jake instinctively knew what she was thinking.

"You're right, if you would have stayed, you probably would have been dead right now too." "It sounds like the hit on your husband was a professional." "Everything is going to be alright, Mattie." "We'll find your daughter." "First we have to find a safe place for you to stay until we can figure this thing out." Jake wanted so badly to hold Mattie and stroke her hair gently. He mourned with her for her loss and her tumultuous situation. What do you say to a grieving widow who just lost her daughter too, he thought.

All Jake could come up with was some half-assed promise he would find her daughter. Great, he thought, I'm real convincing, He put his hand over hers, gazing into her teary and tired eyes. "We'll get Melina back, I promise." "Let's get out of here." "We'll go back to my place and figure out what to do." Mattie responded with a forced grin and nodded her head.

They drove off and she put her head on Jake's shoulder while Taylor Dayne's shelter was softly playing on the radio. Jake was Mattie's guardian angel she thought. He was rescuing her from the monster who was destroying her life as she knew it. He was her shelter and protector. She finally took a deep breath of relief. No more thinking, she was exhausted and finally drifted off to sleep. Her body was limp and tired from running and crying. She felt drained from all the emotions of worry and fear and terror for her daughter. She wondered if she would ever see her baby again.

Jake sang quietly, "Honey, I'll be your shelter, careful not to wake her. He just hoped he wouldn't screw this up for Mattie. She was obviously torn apart from the death of her husband and her daughter's kidnapping. Finding out that the Governor used a hit man to kill his opponent was big, he thought. Sure, Jake wanted some action, but he knew they were in over their heads. Jake wondered if the Governor had planned to set up Mattie all along, especially since he was acting strange that day. It doesn't make sense, he thought. Mattie was just his aide, they were supposedly friends, he was like a father figure to her.

Jake had a lot of thinking to do, so he turned down the radio to try and piece things together like a good private eye would do. Tomorrow is another day, he thought, hope it's better than this one.

CHAPTER 5

Governor Sam Waters wiped the sweat from his brow. "We've got to get these pictures from Mattie or my life is over." The order was given to the Governor's hit man, Antonio Scollini. "Find her, get me those pictures!" "Can you handle that?" "Why didn't you wait for her to get home and get those pictures?" Scollini seemed annoyed at the Governor's inquisition, but he was getting paid well.

"My partner called and said they found a body, so I had to leave so no one would suspect anything." "I believe it was Seth Jenkins, Governor." "Remember him?" "Scollini cackled to himself. "Nobody likes a wise guy Scollini." "Don't worry, I'll take care of everything." "One more thing, the Governor hesitated. "She's been like a daughter to me, make sure she doesn't suffer and I don't want to know the details." "You got that!" "Yeah, Scollini retorted, I got that." "My sources say she's with that pretty boy Jake Estevan in Beaver Dam."

"You'll have to take care of them both and no witnesses." "I don't want anything that could lead back to me." "Make sure it's clean." "Like dust in the wind, Governor." The plan was simple like a well-oiled machine. Rub out Seth Jenkins, no competition, no problems. The Governor was well liked by his constituents. Sam Waters was sweet and sincere and charming to everyone. When Sam spoke, people paid attention.

Sam wasn't counting on trouble from Mattie McGraw. It was all a big mistake and it was going to cost him big. The people of Kentucky had no idea what darkness laid within Governor Sam Waters. Sam was determined not to fall into the life his father led, which was miserable and short as a coal miner. Luckily, Sam was smart and he graduated top of his class at Western Kentucky University with a business degree. Sam was an American dream come true.

He was extremely successful with his construction company who earned millionaire status by the age of 35. The political bug bit him in school when he started working campaigns in college. The power these politicos had was like an aphrodisiac, mesmerizing him into a trance. Sam had plenty of bucks and let his money do the talking. He could make things happen. Fifty-thousand to the churches of Louisville could buy you a lot of friends in the community and Sam wasn't taking any chances with his first run for Governor. So, what if the votes were illegal, he wasn't getting his hands dirty.

He let his best friend Lenny take care of the little things, that was his job. Sam Waters wasn't about to let go of his job as Governor so easily. He loved being in the limelight. He was determined to change Kentucky's status to the other states and to the world. He wanted pay raises for teachers, student testing and a higher rating for Kentucky schools.

Sam wholeheartedly believed he could change that. The unions loved their Governor and stood by him avidly. The first few years went well for the Governor. He was a doer, not a yellow-belly and became known as "I'm Sam, I am, I can do anything you think I can." After the Governor passed the we-care law, that protected domestically abused women, he became a super-hero.

A lot however, can change in a few years. The political pendulum was swinging to the right, far right. It started with the Republicans taking over the White House and unseating 12 Democrats in the Senate. The mood of America was changing as well. Americans were angry and bitter over the terrorist attack on the U.S. Embassy in Beijing. Americans were calling for swift justice and the Republicans were all too happy to answer their pleas.

There were also numerous threats from terrorists worldwide to strike U.S. grounds leaving many Americans uneasy about their own defense. The Conservatives had one leg up because of conceptions. The good ole boys were tough on defense and much more patriotic than the bleeding-heart liberals. The numbers in the Governor's polls began dropping almost six months before the election. Forget that the we-care law was a huge success, protecting hundreds of abused women.

People seemed to forget about Governor Sam raising Kentucky's education standards and bringing jobs to the Commonwealth of Kentucky. The people of Kentucky were gripped in fear with the rest of the nation and the good ole' boys harped on all those fears. Life just wasn't playing fair and Sam decided he would take the election any way he could. He found himself reminiscing about the past two years with Mattie McGraw.

She was like a pit bull, fighting hard to get the Governor elected in his first bid for Governor. Mattie came along when Sam was looking for a strong woman's voice, the votes, and the backing. Working for domestically abused women, Mattie was a perfect fit to his staff. He liked her the first time he saw her, she was a fighter. She had brains and brass with legal knowledge. The women of Kentucky loved Mattie McGraw. She wasn't afraid of anything and was very passionate about protecting them from their abusers.

Mattie was going to be greatly missed by everyone. He tried to put her out of his mind and out of his heart, but he truly loved her. She had to be dealt with however, she was like loaded dynamite that could take him down forever. Governor was always generous with his best friends, but he dealt with his enemies or anyone that posed a threat maliciously and methodically.

Mattie was no longer his supporter, she was a serious threat being alive somewhere in Kentucky roaming free. He hoped Scollini would find her soon and eliminate his problem. He also hoped and prayed that God would forgive him for killing her.

CHAPTER 6

Jake and Mattie arrived in Beaver Dam after a long endless road led them to their destination. They were both exhausted and ready to pass out. Beaver Dam was extremely cold in November, but so beautiful at night. As they drove downtown, the Christmas decorations glittered with lights streaming from one end of the square to the other. Downtown looked like a winter wonderland with enormous candy canes hanging from the light posts. The small town was deserted and quiet.

Great place for escape from unknown madman with guns Jake thought. They'll never find us here. Jake was relieved to be on his own ground, he knew best, so he could protect himself and Mattie. Only a few days left until the election. Soon the Governor Sam I Am, I Can Do Anything You Think I Can would be Governor again unless he was exposed.

Mattie woke up the next morning with the hangover from hell. Her head was pounding and she felt dizzy. She felt sick with fear and anxiety that the monster was going to get away with everything. She took a deep breath. Her thoughts were with Ben and Melina. "Where is she, where's my baby?" The hairs on the back of her neck were standing, momentarily paralyzing her by the pain of her loss. Holding on to Melina's bear calmed her briefly and spurned hope of seeing her daughter again.

She dreamed all night that Ben was calling her and he was reaching out to her, but as soon as she got close to his ethereal being he vaporized in front of her. All she could remember were his words. "Find our daughter Mattie and bring her back." It all seemed surreal, like it never happened, but unfortunately, she remembered holding Ben in her lap with no response. She knew Ben was dead and her daughter was out there somewhere and she would never give up till she found her.

She felt a strong, large hand on the back of her neck and turned to see Jake wasn't looking so hot either. The bags under his eyes were dark and he was still dressed in his clothes from the night before. "Did you get some sleep last night?" "Not much, I kept dreaming about Ben." "He seemed so real." "I kept seeing him and he was reaching out to me shouting I'm here Mattie." "I'm here." "I'll never leave you." "Then I was running to him, but before I could get to him, he kept disappearing into thin air."

"I kept hearing Melina cry Momma, momma and I couldn't find her." "I just kept reliving that moment when she was being taken from me." "I kept thinking if I could have gotten there five or ten minutes earlier, I could have stopped all this from happening." "If you had gotten there earlier, you'd be dead too." "And you have to know that Mattie." "I guess I don't know anymore." "What I do know is that I've got to tell the Attorney General and make sure he has the envelope I sent him." Jax will help us, I know he will." "I need some courage first and a couple of aspirin."

Mattie licked her lips and cleared her throat. Jax and Mattie were good friends for a long time. He begged her time and again to leave the Governor's office and to work for him. Jax was always suspicious of the Governor and his dealings. He could never get the hard evidence against him. Jax would be abhorred by the pictures, but he'll understand. Jax hated the Governor. Jax knew the Governor had bought illegal votes during his first campaign run, but could never prove it.

Jack finally backed off the investigation since he was coming up for reelection himself. He vowed someday that he would get Sam I Am and send him to prison where he belonged.

Jake handed Mattie a hot cup of coffee and she downed it in one gulp. The bitter taste took her aback at first, but it wasn't so bad. It really woke her up. Mattie reached for the phone and dialed Jax's office. The call went right through to his secretary. "May I ask who is calling?"

She hesitated at first then blurted out, Mattie McGraw." "Mattie sweetheart, what's going on?" "Jax, just listen to me." "I sent you a package, did you get it?" "A package, just a minute Mattie." "Clarice did I get a package from Mattie McGraw?" His secretary's voice echoed in the background. "Here it is, do you want me to open it?" "No, Jax replied, bring it to me." "Wait, wait!" Mattie's heart was pounding. "Before you open it, Oh my God." Jax's mouth dropped he was horrified by the pictures.

In the background, the news was on with a special bulletin. News reporter Julie Welch with channel WEVV was seated stiffly delivering the shocking news. "Gubernatorial candidate Seth Jenkins was found murdered. His body was found in the trunk of his car. In Lexington, renowned lawyer Ben McGraw was also found shot to death in his home. Police are on the lookout for Mattie McGraw the wife of Ben McGraw.

She is a person of interest and wanted for questioning in relation to the death of Seth Jenkins, Ben McGraw, and the disappearance of her infant daughter Melina McGraw. There was dead silence on the phone. Mattie sat helpless as she heard the bulletin come across the television at the same time Jax heard it. "Mattie what did you do, where are you?" "Why Jax I didn't do it!" "The pictures!" "They were sent to the Governor's office!" "He killed Seth and Ben!" "You have to believe me!"

She tried to explain in a calm voice, but she was frantic to make him listen. "I came home and Ben was dead." "Then I saw Melina being taken away by some woman whose vehicle I recognized at the Governor's office!" "The Governor had the pictures sent to his office, knowing full well that I would open them!" "I took care of all his incoming mail." "Believe me, I was as shocked as you are now looking at those horrifying pictures!"

"He asked me not to tell anyone, that he was desperate to hold on to the Governor's office." "I panicked and ran with them." "I was taking them to my husband because I knew he would know what to do." "By the time I got home he was dead and Melina was kidnapped." "Everything I've told you is the truth Jax, you know that I loved my husband and my life with Ben and Melina!"

"Sure, sure Mattie......uh-huh." "I called because you were my last hope Jax." "Don't you believe me!" "Mattie, I don't know all the details, but if you'll just turn yourself in, maybe I can help you." Mattie didn't like the tone of his voice. "He doesn't believe me!" He was one of them. Jake grabbed the phone out of Mattie's frozen hand "He didn't believe you, did he?" Mattie just shook her head and burst into tears. Jax was her last hope to clear her name, now he was siding with the monster.

"I'm also a fugitive, the police are after me!" "I've got to get out of here!" Mattie sprang up to run out of the cabin. Jake was fast and stopped her in her tracks. "Wait, you can't go out there!" "You've got a contract on your head, you can't go anywhere!" "I can't just sit here and let them run my name through the mud, I've got to do something Jake!" "Melina's out there somewhere and we're going to find her, but you've got to keep yourself safe first!" Jake held Mattie tightly reassuring her as if it were already over with. It wouldn't last long however, danger was right around the corner, by the name of Antonio Scollini. Things were about to get far worse than they could ever imagine.

CHAPTER 7

Scollini pulled up to Jake's cabin and reached for his silencer. He had been searching all throughout the night for the two outlaws. By that point, he wasn't in the mood for any of their games. The orders from Sam were clear, "Kill Mattie McGraw and anyone associated with her at the time, make the whole thing look like a suicide." In his intent, he hoped to frame Mattie for the murder of Seth Jenkins. Sam could see the headlines now, *"Overzealous Secretary Takes Out Governor's Opponent for Personal Benefit," "Husband Becomes Innocent Victim in the Crossfire of Diabolical Plans, "Child Missing, Never to Be Found."* Governor Sam would definitely take care of that.

The plan was perfect, everything wrapped up neatly in a forged suicide note, the well written words of a psychopathic killer. The note would read:

"TO WHOM IT MAY CONCERN,

I'm so sorry for all the pain I've caused. Words can't express the sorrow I feel for each families' loss. I owe a great deal to the Governor for giving me the opportunity of a lifetime. I worked for a wonderful and very understanding man. I was misguided in thinking I was helping him maintain his position as Governor, as well as my job. Seth Jenkins did not deserve to die so inhumanly.

After my husband found out I was responsible for Seth's murder, it was all over. I panicked, I had no choice but to cover my tracks. I truly loved my husband, he was loving, but killing him was my deepest regret. I also killed my daughter so she would not have to go through life without a mother and a father. My heart breaks, because I will never get to hold her again. I am so truly sorry. As for my child, she is in a far better place now with the angels. I pray God will forgive me.

Madeline L. McGraw.

This was perfect, Sam thought. The words of an emotionally disturbed woman who obviously needed help. No one could ever trace the murders back to him. A poorly deranged woman, who confused right from wrong. His plan to turn poor, sociopath Mattie McGraw into a victim that the public would eventually feel sympathetic for, after all the shock of the events wore off. He decided to at least give her some dignity with her death. She would be remembered as a sad, pathetic woman who was very, very sick. Sam felt a brief shadow of sadness come over him. He didn't care whether this was wrong or right, he knew he had to maintain his governorly status. He knew how to make things happen. He was ruthless and no one was going to take his trophy life away from him.

Scollini had his orders to fulfill, laughing at how much of a coward the Governor was. He nearly rolled over laughing when he received the orders in the first place. It was his job, he'd do it however he damned well pleased. A devious grin grew on his face as the adrenaline circulated through his body. His go to music was AC/DC, as he played *Highway to Hell* on repeat, since most of the radio music annoyed him. He liked the intensely loud, chaotic music from bands such as Megadeth. This music took him into the game for the kill. Scollini liked a good kill. He knew he'd pay for his crimes someday and there was a place in hell with his name on it.

He wanted to know where his protector was when he suffered at the hands of his manic father. Every day it was a different form of torture for Scollini. Some days he would be trapped in the dark, cold closet for several hours only hearing his mother's screams. At other times he was forced to sleep outside in the doghouse with no food or water. He did not deserve such treatment for speaking out of line. After being subjected to years of abuse, Scollini and his mother finally caught a break. One night, his father went too far over the edge, trying to drown his mother in the bathtub. He heard the desperate gasps for air, as she struggled for her life. Scollini grabbed a vase, slamming it onto his father's head. His father was knocked out instantaneously from impact. He reached for the phone, shoving it into his mother's face. "No more," he said coldly. "Call the police." The police arrived within the hour, taking away his father and the beatings stopped. It was too late, Scollini thought. The sins of the father were now on the child and he would make the world pay for his torment. He especially hated his mother for being weak. Why couldn't she protect him or herself for that matter? In that moment, he had no use for weak human beings.

He was a super force, with a gun at hand he wielded the power so damn well. The top marksman in his class at the academy, no one could compete with him or come close. This gave Scollini huge satisfaction.

He slipped on his black leathered gloves and cocked his gun. It was time to play the game he loved so much, and he reveled in that. He was ready for the game to begin and oh what fun he would have.

Jake felt uneased about wanting to hold Mattie in his arms. He briefly released her from his grip, something was wrong. His gut instincts were right, smelling trouble from a mile away. His intuitions also kept him safe in his line of work, especially with the usual suspicions of cheating spouses. He heard movements outside the cabin, something was out there. Jake looked concerned and it casted doubts on whether this would be a safe place to hide. "Shhh, stay here out of sight!" "Don't move!" "I'm going to investigate the noises coming from outside." He had hoped that bringing Mattie out to the cabins would buy them sometime while they figured out a plan. Time was fleeting, and he knew it. He reached for his gun and walked cautiously to the front door to look out the window. An unmarked police car was sitting in the driveway. He wondered where the policemen were, the ones with the bullhorns, the guns, and the waiting signals to attack the two fugitives. Someone else was already in the house, and he knew it, but couldn't pin them anywhere. This wasn't the police, this was someone more ominous. He had a sixth sense for these things. He turned around, but wasn't fast enough as Scollini coldcocked him in the head. The force of the blow was so hard it put Jake out cold. His body hit the floor and he never knew what hit him.

Mattie wanted to yell out Jake's name, but decided to keep quiet in case someone was already there. Before she entered the living room, she saw a long slender figure stepping out of the shadows. She jumped with fear that paralyzed her for the moment.

"Hello Mattie," said Scollini, wearing the darkest expression on his face. His eyes looked black. "Remember me? You should, since I remember you perfectly."

Mattie knew him well, and feared for her life as to what he would do next. She remembered him from high school, all the times he tormented her friends, and used his stature to gain power over others. She feared as she was his next victim. Mattie scoped the room for any signs of Jake. Her heart sank. "I've taken care of your little friend." "He won't be bothering us."

Mattie stammered helplessly, "I can get you those pictures, anything really, just please don't hurt me." She begged with outstretched arms, backing away from him slowly. This amused Scollini for a moment, and he sprung forward, grabbing her and drawing her closer to him. She couldn't fight the tight grip on her arm.

"I don't care about any damn pictures," he said with no expression. "I've been searching for you all night Mattie, pretty, pretty Mattie. If you learned to keep your nose out of everyone else's business," he spoke in hushed tones.

"You're the girl who wouldn't give me the time of day back in high school. I see you're just another one of Jake Estevan's sluts!" "How pathetic. Looks like he can't help you now, can he?" He grabbed her hair and pulled her head back.

"Please," she screamed. "Stop this already, I won't tell anyone. I have money, just name your price already." There was no reasoning with him. He smacked her hard across the face, throwing her across the floor. She was dazed momentarily. No man had ever abused her like that before.

"We're going to have a little fun first," he taunted.

Mattie didn't like the sound of that, her adrenaline pumping. He began walking towards her fallen body slowly. "Time to play with the prey, and torment the bitch," he thought.

Mattie was drawing a blank, hoping something would come to her from those self-defense classes she took.

"Killing your husband was absolutely boring," he teased. "He didn't even put up a real fight." Scollini cackled. "It was pitiful seeing him beg, telling me to take everything I wanted and leave. He's not a real man, he was weak just like his wife."

Scollini continued to mock Ben, "Please don't kill me, I'll give you everything I have."

At that point, Mattie was furious with him and determined not to be his next victim. "You're pathetic," she spat. Tauntingly, "no one on this Earth gives a damn about whether you live or die Antonio."

She kicked him in the crotch with all of her strength. It worked, as her tormenter dropped on his knees, aching in pain. Mattie knocked him winded, as he gasped for air. This was a good time to break free. Her reflexes gave way and she leapt for the door, but it was no use. Scollini grabbed her leg, trying to jerk away from him. She knew her life depended on it. She kicked him in the face and he finally released her. She bolted for the door, there was Jake pointing his .38 like she was one of his targets. Jake pushed Mattie back as she turned to see Scollini alive for the last time. He raised his arm to fire a shot at them both, but Jake fired the first rounds, successfully keeping a clear shot for his chest. Scollini was swaying from side to side, and Jake plugged him again. Scollini fell to the floor dead.

CHAPTER 8

"There, there now sweetheart." "Everything will be fine, as she patted Melina on her back and pulled the blanket over the baby. "Soon you'll have new parents and they'll take very good care of you." "Poor child with no parents, Rosa thought. Rosa wondered how a mother could just go crazy and kill like a wild animal. "Don't worry darling, you'll never have to see that wicked woman ever again."

Governor Sam would take care of everything. The call was already made to Switzerland. A childless couple the Governor had met on a ski vacation. They were the most annoying people he had ever met. Their life was an open book from the tax evasion charges, swinging lifestyle, and finally he remembered they were not able to have children. He almost threw the business card away, but it really came in handy, perfect he thought.

A childless couple who desperately wanted a child, sure they were idiots, he thought. They were very, very rich idiots. There would be no background checks and investigations into their life. It would be easy. One-hundred thousand up front for baby Melina and tomorrow the child would be delivered by Nanny Rosa. The simple well-planned scheme Governor Sam had concocted was falling apart unbeknownst to him. The Governor was all smiles. He kicked his feet upon his desk and let his imagination run away with him.

Governor Sam could envision election night. "Governor Sam, I am, I can do anything you think I can, has done it again." "Governor Sam has won by a landslide." In the background, he ignored the news reports, "But where is baby Melina, she is nowhere to be found."

It was time to go, Jake was nervous. There was no safe place for them anymore until this was all cleaned up. "I just remember the car that took Melina away." Mattie muttered excitedly. "Are you sure?" "Yes, I'm sure." It was so clear to Mattie. How could she have let this one get by. She had been to the Governor's mansion so many times. "Rosa, it was Rosa!" Mattie remembered the cold-dark face that greeted her with every visit. "Let's go get her!" Jake shook his head.

Sure, he wanted some excitement in his life, but a fugitive on the run didn't fit with his plans. "Alright, I've got an idea, hold that thought!" "I'll be right back." Jake walked to the hall closet and grabbed two dark dresses out. His secret joke was the closet of shame. There was every disguise perfect for his line of his work. From the slutty prostitute to the three-piece sharp dressed business man's suit. Jake almost giggled when he saw it.

He made the perfect hooker with his gold lame dress jacket and stiletto pumps and a blonde wig. Even the Johns didn't know he was a Joe. Damn people could be stupid, Jake thought. The nun outfits would be perfect, no one would suspect a thing. "Who would suspect a sweet nun?" "We'll need disguises if we're going to make a call at the mansion." Mattie wasn't convinced, she just didn't feel like playing dress up. "We're going out into the world as nuns, are you kidding me?"

"Nuns Jake?" "Isn't this a stretch even for you?" "Take it or leave it!" "Half of the police force in Kentucky are looking for us Mattie!" Mattie rolled her eyes and grabbed the dress. She was in no mood to argue. This is insane she thought. "Who in their right minds is going to believe we're nuns?" They put the dresses on quickly. Time was running out. There was no turning back now. "I'll just clean things up here and we'll go." Mattie knew the thing that had to be taken care of.

Scollini was in the corner motionless. Just looking at him made her sick. "Jake, I'm so sorry, don't go there Mattie." "He would have killed us both and we know it." "I'll protect you no matter what." "I've got this one." Jake picked up his lifeless body and laid Scollini out on the Oriental carpet. The body was much heavier than Jake anticipated, it nearly threw his back out. A letter fell out of his pocket and he kicked it out of the way. Cautiously he took the gun and laid it aside. He rolled the carpet over Scollini and put the body in a freezer in the garage.

The thought of a dead body in his house really made Jake sick. Meanwhile, Mattie picked up the crinkle paper and began to read. With every word, she cringed and held her stomach. It was the most morose thing she had ever laid eyes on. Mattie was furiously reading her suicide note, holding it with a death grip. "What is it Mattie?" She was speechless. The plan was laid out before her very eyes. "My suicide letter, he set me up!" "He was going to frame me for the murders anyway!" Mattie was filled with rage. This was no longer the sweet kind-hearted old gentleman she knew anymore. The tables have turned, she thought.

No more sweet, dear clueless Mattie. Anger filled her and she realized Sam would stop at nothing to remain in office as Governor. She was livid and ready to fight back. It was time to fight back and take what was hers again. She knew she couldn't bring Ben back, but he wouldn't die in vain either. It was time for revenge in the bluegrass served up cold by Mattie McGraw. It was time for justice Mattie style! "Let's go Jake, he's not going to get away with this!"

Jake and Mattie marched out the door like soldiers heading out to war. It was time to combat the monster who wiped her life out like an intrepid tornado. Husband and daughter gone. Reputation, who cares she thought. They were the good guys fighting the bad. Nothing was going to stop them now, except the click of a .38 pointed right in their faces.

They were completely taken by surprise and the cold hard stare of a very unhappy police officer. It was Lil'J Newton. He was sent by Jax McCarthy. He knew Mattie was in trouble and really wanted to help her. "Going somewhere folks?" Mattie and Jake raised their hands and held their breath. Lil'J was an old friend of Mattie and Jake's at Ohio County High School. He was almost completely unrecognizable now.

Back in high school Lil'J weighed over 300 pounds which didn't quite seem to fit the stature of his small boyish face. Lil'J was adored by everyone. He had a real sweet nature. Lil'J was the class clown and was always making people laugh. Mattie adored Lil'J too. She was so proud of him for fulfilling his dream to be a police officer. She admired him so much for that. Lil'J had dropped two-hundred pounds and looked like a completely different person.

He had beautiful, wavy blonde hair which accentuated his florescent blue eyes and bright smile. She was taken aback by his stellar good looks. Lil'J was quite handsome. Mattie prayed he was the good cop. Nothing like Scollini, who abused his position. "You can both put your hands down now." As he rolled his eyes and shook his head. "I'm glad I found you." He put his gun away and grabbed Mattie for a huge bear hug. Jake was completely confused. "I was sent by Jax McCarthy."

Mattie backed away frightened. "Don't be afraid Mattie." "Jax and me, we're the good guys, remember that." He placed his arm on her shoulder for reassurance.

He could sense she was rattled. "He didn't believe me when I called him." "I don't know who to trust anymore." "We'll get to the bottom of this Mattie!" "I'm innocent, I didn't do any of these horrible things!" "I was set up by the Governor!" "I believe you Mattie." "We've been investigating Sam." "We found the private investigator who took the pictures of Seth Jenkins with his mistress."

"He said a few weeks ago a man paid him to take the pictures of Seth and his mistress, you know follow him around." Lil'J pulled out a picture from his pocket. "Do you recognize this man Mattie?" It was a drawing of Antonio Scollini. "I sure do." "We thought you might be in danger, so I was sent to protect you." "We know him too well, he just tried to kill us." "Where is he now?" "He's in the garage in the freezer." Jake said non-chalantly.

"He banged me on the head with his gun and knocked me out." "I was out cold for a few minutes." "Then when I woke up he was throwing Mattie around like a rag doll." "I overheard him tell Mattie he killed Ben and he couldn't wait to kill her too." This guy was a complete sociopath." "If I hadn't awoken when I did, we wouldn't be standing here right now." "Is he dead?" "Yeah, he's as dead as they get." "Lil'J couldn't help notice Mattie's bruised face. "Wait right here." He walked carefully into the garage with his gun raised and slowly opened the freezer door.

He remembered the bastard who sent him to the hospital, beaten like a whipped dog. Lil'J wasn't taking any chances this time. Three broken ribs, broken nose, and a concussion that put him out for days. His heart was racing as he unfolded the Oriental rug that covered Scollini's body. There lay Scollini, the tormentor. He was dead just as Mattie and Jake verified. Lil'J hated Scollini. Guys like him give good cops a bad name. He was the bad seed that could only root evil. He took a deep breath of relief when he realized yep, the tormentor is really dead.

He had to fight the urge to kick Scollini, but he wanted to so badly. Lil'J motioned for Jake and Mattie to come inside and they sat down at the kitchen table. Mattie told Lil'J the whole story as she poured her heart out to him. Lil'J seemed satisfied with her answers after questioning her carefully for an hour. Lil'J believed in Mattie and she trusted him too. "If you were investigating the Governor, why hasn't he been arrested?" Lil'J looked ashamed, but adamant. "We didn't have enough evidence to make it stick." "We thought he was going to blackmail Seth Jenkins out of running because he was losing." "It looks like Governor Sam had other plans for Seth Jenkins.

"Melina…she choked on her words for a minute. "She's at the Governor's mansion, I know it." "They've got her J." 'I want her back." "Don't worry Mattie, we'll get your daughter back." "But what's with the nun outfits?" "Did you really think you could pull that off?" He said with a smirk on his face. 'Forget the outfits!"

"If we don't get Melina today, she may not be found tomorrow." "She's right, the Governor has to get rid of her so there are no questions about the baby." Jake didn't want to cause Mattie more grief, but it had to be said. The strategizing began. This was like old times for Mattie. Sitting around the war tables like war generals issuing orders where the attacks would begin. It was decided that all three would go to the Governor's mansion.

The nun outfits might come in handy after all. Jake and Lil'J decided Mattie would have to hide out in the backseat of the car from everyone and everything that could expose her as the fugitive on the run. Jake and Lil'J would go to the door for donations for the church. Jake would create a disturbance, which he was great at. He was a legend from faking stomachaches to full-fledged strokes. Jake was a pro. Lil'J would get in and search for the baby, since he knew the floor plan top to bottom.

Normally, with all the information Lil'J had on the Governor, everything would have gone down. The arrest would have been made and this would have been over. But Lil'J knew if they struck too soon, that Sam might panic and take his own life, the baby's or both. He wasn't willing to take that chance. The plan was made, get Melina first and take out Sam in handcuffs. Lil'J knew this was risky and could end his career with the police force if anything went wrong. Lil'J felt compelled to help Mattie and he was hoping for a happy ending.

Jake was ready, he hadn't seen this much action in years. He grabbed his extra bullets and his rosary beads and said a quick prayer. He was a little scared too, but he couldn't show Mattie. Lil'J and his commandos as they were named, took care of Scollini. They knew if Governor Sam was on to them in anyway, their whole plan would backfire and Melina could be lost forever. He decided to forge ahead with the plan, but with extreme caution.

Mattie's life flashed before her eyes. It was grim and dark, something out of a bad women's movie." "Prisoner 138792056." "No husband, no daughter." The guard smiled at her wickedly. "Welcome to your new home, ha, ha!" "You're locked up life!" "We threw away the keys just for you, Mattie the Madhatter!" "You're never getting out of here ever!" "But I'm innocent I keep telling you!" "You have to believe me!" she pleaded. She slowly reached her hand out between the bars as the thunderous cracks of laughter surrounded her. They mocked her as she tried to close her ears off from the guttural voices. "But I'm innocent, I'm innocent!"

"Lights out for Mattie the Madhatter, as the lights went dim she could only see her shadow from the corner she squatted into from fear. It was all over. She immediately opened her eyes, it was a horrible dream. "I won't let this happen to me."

The monster has to be taken down. Melina's life was at stake. Jake just hoped they would get there in time to save Melina from whatever fate the Governor had already decided for the small child. Lil'J was truly concerned for Melina too, he knew what a ruthless man Governor Sam could be.

CHAPTER 9

Kentuckians were in shock over the untimely death of Seth Jenkins. The Governor was at a crossroads. The end of the election was nearing and still he had some voters to win over. It was unheard of for a deceased candidate to win usually, but Sam left no stones unturned. He played the sympathetic face at the press conference.

"Even though we had opposite philosophies about to govern Kentucky, we both shared a great dream. To be the best Governor we can be. To govern an incredible state with the highest of intentions. To do great things and take his beautiful state to greater horizons. To educate our youths, bringing higher paying jobs, and to unite Kentuckians."

There wasn't a dry eye when Sam finished his speech, tugging at the heart strings of people. He won the press over and he knew it. He had no trouble reminding Kentuckians how great and prosperous the last four years had been. There were raises for extremely underpaid teachers and the we-care program, and the numbers fell out of his mouth generously.

He promised even better things to come. Yes, the future looked bright if Kentucky could only elect the charming Governor for another term. Sam had most of his constituents in the bag, it was the remaining 30% he was fearful of. He was a man that could answer the toughest questions, and became an expert on campaigning strategies.

"Had it not been for the untimely death of your competitor Seth Jenkins, do you think you would have had this much success in your reelection?" asked one reporter during the press conference.

Sam placed a great deal of faith in his people, expressing his undying concerns for the future of his state. His promise to do the impossible, bringing better jobs to Kentucky so that families could provide a better standard of living, and turn back their trust in him. He had more campaigning to do, bringing in the heavy artilleries. He wasn't just hoping for the final victory, he wanted a grand slam.

While boasting his own pursuits, he imagined how things could've been. He imagined a little girl off in the distance playing with her oversized blue ball. "Melina, time to go home," he said in his mind. He would've raised her if things would've turned out differently. He swept up Melina, embracing her with a tight hug, and kissing her tiny, little red cheeks. "I'm sorry about your mother, sweetie. You'll be fine now that Uncle Sam's here for you." He smiled at her briefly, while releasing her to resume playing. "You'll lead a happy life, this I promise," he said as she ran off into the hall to fetch it. "Good luck, dear." He said as he came back to reality.

Pangs of guilt tore at his soul. He wasn't willing to let his emotions get to his senses now. He felt like a monster acting the way he did, and for doing this to Mattie. He was separating her from her little girl, but someone had to pay and it sure wasn't going to be him. In his mind, he could hear the echoes of an older Melina crying for her mother, "Momma," she cried over and over. "This will soon pass," he thought, trying to justify his actions. Kentucky needed his vision, his clarity, and his guidance. "They would be at a loss without me."

The news had a field day with Mattie's story, making coverage nationwide. From *The Tonight Show*, she was earned the nickname *Mattie the Madhatter*. From the host's opening dialogue, *"You got a political opponent that you just wanna wipe away? No problem, call Mattie the Madhatter. It would seem that no problems too big or too small for the Madhatter."* On another show politicos were fiercely fighting about the deeply disturbed psychopath. The men however, were furious and screaming for her head on a platter. Bill McGuff, the host of this show gave his usual remarks. He rolled his eyes with a grimaced face, and smirked. Somehow Bill knew how to get what he wanted from a restless audience and how to stir up heated argumentative debates between the panelist. "Catch that bitch and fry her up," he scoffed. The audience went wild. They booed, jeering as the panelists were at each other's throats. Bill wore his gapped smile wickedly on his thin lips waiting for a Jerry Springer moment when one of the panelists would lose it and bitch slapped one another.

Mattie wasn't aware of her newly found fame from New York to Los Angeles to Washington D.C. The headlines she read, "*Why DID Mattie Go Mad*," "*Where's the Baby?*" "*A Dark and Revengeful Night in the Bluegrass.*" All the national attention was unflattering and greatly unappreciated. Thousands of supporters attended the funeral of Seth Jenkins. One attendee, his wife Nicole was furious and heartbroken. She portrayed the weeping widow at his funeral perfectly. She clinched her handkerchief tightly, wiping away the runny mascara in her tearful eyes. She walked up to the open casket, "Goodbye my darling, she said as she walked away. Seth's family was deeply touched by her affectionate displays for him. Little did they know she was the black widow who fought for his untimely demise.

It received the attention of the Governor when his numbers were dwindling in the polls. Nicole Jenkins was relieved by Seth's murder, finally in contempt with him gone from the picture. Seth was a control freak, controlling every move she made. He would tell her how to dress, how to speak in public engagements, and decided who she could be friends with. In her own way, she was a prisoner trapped in a dark castle with nowhere to run. She could never live up to the standards he set for her, and she was more than willing to move on with her life, especially with her own secrets.

The only thing keeping her from plummeting was her affair with Maco, their Italian gardener of five years. She loved his olive colored skin, his musky natural smell, and the way his thick accent said her name while making passionate love in the rose bushes. She wanted to someday to meet this Mattie McGraw and thank her personally for her newfound freedom.

Headlines shocked supporters when Nicole fledged her full support to Sam and his campaign. Nicole didn't care to be a Governor's wife. She felt no loyalty to anyone but herself. As she stepped into her white limousine, she reflected on her accomplishments on the ride home. Her happiness was just around the corner. She anxiously waited to be held by her lover's strong arms that would make her forget. She wanted to be loved, truly loved the way a woman needed to be loved by a passionate man. While in a way Seth provided for her, nice clothes, fancy house, and a baby, she grew tired of the motherly responsibilities, much to Seth's chagrin. She had bigger plans, being a mother and somebody's wife weren't included. As the limousine pulled into the driveway, she thought, This is where my life begins and sorrow ends.

CHAPTER 10

T hings were quiet at the Governor's mansion with no signs of Melina to be found. Lil J and Jake searched every square inch of the house. Passing from each room to room, everything seemed in place. The Victorian paintings on the wall, the freshly scrubbed marble floors encompassing the banquet room that served the Governor's fundraising events, everything looked superb.

The only remaining shred of evidence they could link to Melina was a child's blue ball. Everyone in Sam's staff were questioned in great lengths. Their attentions were focused on preparing the mansion for a celebratory victory party in Sam's honor. Kitchen staff carefully planned the menu with shrimp scampi, crab legs, duck al'orange, and cheesecake of every variety. This was a feast fit for a king and his royal subjects. Lil J' and Jake searched, hoping their last place to look would have all the clues necessary. The broke into Sam's office, looking for any signs that could link Sam to the murders. All they could find was Sam and his strategist's plan for the undecided voters. From the scribbles on his pad, Louisville seemed to be the choice for a grand victory.

The boys felt hopelessness as they were annoyed with the grand preparations being made on the Governor's behalf. They felt waves of grief as they let Mattie down. Both of them had to decide who would break the news to her that their daughter was untraceably gone. Jake was given the task to break the news to her that Melina was untraceably gone. Lil' J felt way over his head with this situation, reaching for his phone to call his superiors. Both knew Melina was out there, and that

Sam was devious, but surely, he wouldn't harm a child. He knew it was time to dig deeper and send out the troops.

Mattie sat huddled in Lil J's car for what seemed like hours in a matter of moments. She grew restless from the anticipation as she fought the urges of busting out of that car. Her hands trembled as she touched over the car handle. She rationalized the consequences of this idea. Someone could identify her and then this whole plan would be over. She pictured herself being carried off in handcuffs, sent to prison for the rest of her days, paying for the crimes of that heinous monster.

"No," she muttered under her breath. "Resist the urge to help them. Fight your instincts McGraw," she said trying to assure herself. "They will bring her to me and this nightmare will be over." She trusted her friends, knowing if anyone could successfully find her daughter, it would be those two. She quivered, wondering what was taking so long, worrying that they were discovered. She had a worried look on her face, peeking through the window for any signs of them walking out to the car.

Jake slowly walked out to the car, pulling off the headdress to his nun costume. He opened the door, pulling her towards him. He wrapped his arm around her and he sat in the car with her. Her face turned white, as the blood ran out of her cheeks making them colorless and pale. Something was not right. She knew he was hiding something.

"Where the hell is she, Jake," she questioned him.

He hesitated for the right words, but couldn't find them.

"She's gone," he said stoic.

"You're lying to me," she contested.

She grabbed his jacket, looked straight into his eyes for the answers that would satisfy her. "I'm sorry, we did the best we could, searching everything, leaving no stones unturned. She's just not there."

Her hand came out of nowhere and slapped Jake across his face, leaving a red mark. He was trying to be a man and not cry, but tears welled up and he choked up. "Liar," she called him. "You promised me damn it, that you would bring her to me safely," as she began pounding on his chest. "I hate you!" Mattie started slipping on the ground uncontrollably, Jake caught her. Her eyes met his as he held onto her with tears streaming down both their eyes. "I'm sorry baby. I would promise you the world if it would make you smile once more." The whole situation took ahold of Jake. He was usually reserved, never to show too much emotion, his line of work depended on it.

Mattie didn't hear any of his words to comfort her, but rather she was despondent. She knew in her heart the only person she could count on was herself. Sam wasn't going to walk away scott-free after destroying her life. She wasn't looking to be comforted by the man anymore. She stopped crying, took in a deep breath as she calculated her next steps. She knew what to do, seeking justice for Ben, for her daughter, and most importantly herself. Seeking revenge was what she thirsted for as Sam ruined her perfect life. She was cold, numb, yet enraged. "Sorry Jake, I now know what I have to do." She grabbed his gun and pushed him to the ground with a surprised look on his face. "The Governor is going to pay!" She jumped into the car and sped off with him waving his arms to stop, it was too late, she was going on her mission of seek and destroy.

Meanwhile, Nanny Rosa carried Melina as she fussed and cried. The Schwartz couple were delighted when they spotted Nanny Rosa with Melina. The child however, was less than thrilled wanting her mother. Nanny Rosa made the discreet exchange, as Mr. Schwartz handed over a small leather briefcase containing fifty-thousand dollars. Nanny Rosa, hesitated as she held Melina in her arms, She carefully instructed to the couple the baby's needs, health concerns, and even mentioned how the baby responded to Motown music, a note added from Sam. Mrs. Schwartz pulled out a cassette player, prepared for the occasion. She retrieved a homemade cassette tape of Marvin Gaye and the Platters. As soon as the music started playing, Melina took notice and reacted as expected to the sounds of Marvin Gaye. She delighted in the familiarity and clapped her hands as a smile appeared on her face. The couple took a deep sigh of relief and plucked her out of Rosa's hands. They were rushed to catch the next flight to Switzerland, not distracted with the means or the whereabouts of this child they just took.

The couple turned, waved with Melina's hands and hurried off to the airport. Rosa was relieved too. Sam warned her to keep a low profile, reminding her that the stakes were high and an AMBERT alert was issued for that baby. Rosa anxiously wiped the sweat from her brow, proud of the task she accomplished.

The Schwartz's seemed like nice people, she thought as they drove off in a rental car. A bit unconventional, but at least Melina would have a better life. Rosa pulled a red hood over her head to conceal her identity as she briskly walked away. No one ever bothered to question her as a suspect. She felt untouchable. She was more than happy to ruin Mattie's life considering she despised her anyway. She left the airport eased and ready to be praised by Sam. The deed was done, her heart pounding through her chest. She walked a few steps out into the blazing sun when she was caught by surprise. Police cars swarmed the airport, guns drawn and she was ordered to stop. It didn't matter, Melina was on her way to Switzerland, never to be found again. She had no remorse whatsoever as she stood there reflective in her actions, surrounded by a sea of blue uniforms. She knew her time was up, but in her mind, sick and twisted, that baby was safely in the hands of the Schwartz's. She was hesitant, as she sprinted forward, but retracted when she kept hearing "freeze!" from all around.

She sprinted forward as gun shots were drawn. Several shots she darted until two shots hit her, one in the shoulder blade and the other directly into her chest. In that moment, Rosa knew her life was over, struggling, she dropped everything in her grasp, fell instantaneously to the floor. Her body seized as she uttered her final words, "For you Sam, I'll never betray you." The police moved fast, grabbing the cassette tapes from her blood covered body. The tapes she took after the Schwartz's took Melina away.

The rush began, staff members questioned, flight schedules were delayed, passengers were looked over with a fine-tooth comb. The FBI were brought to head this big investigation. Lil J could see the distraught in Mattie's eyes. This experience made him appreciate the life he brought into this world, wanting to run home and hold his children to his chest to let them know they would always be safe. He knew the reality of this situation, somewhere out there Melina McGraw's whereabouts were unknown. He dreamed of bringing Melina home to deliver her into her mother's arms.

"Someday soon," he thought.

The ringing phone in his pocket brought him back to work mode, as he sat motionless briefly. The State police notified him of the kidnapped infant. He could call Mattie, filling her in meticulously with details. No decisions were made yet concerning the Governor. The pictures of Seth Jenkins, the attempt on her life, and Scollini whose body the morgue examiner retrieved, were all puzzles in this sick, twisted game of Sam's. He tied up all the loose ends and pleaded Mattie to drop these charges, to spare his political career.

"This is an innocent woman, no more...she's been through enough in one day," said the Sergeant. "What about them pictures," he quipped.

The fellow officer replied, "I've notified McCarthy, he's off to the house at this very moment."

"Good, we need to keep a lid on this, until we can get the Governor in for questioning." "Nobody goes near him, if he thinks we're onto him he may try to flee the country."

Lil J hung up the phone, relieved heavily a sigh. He felt better that he could restore what was lost from Mattie, her name, and her reputation. He was concerned, Jake and Mattie should've returned by now. As he looked up, the door flew open.

Jake ran in, panting and grabbing his sides, "She's gone Lil'J." "She took your car."

"What?"

"She grabbed my gun and sped off. I think she has revenge on the brain and his name is Sam I am."

"Damn! I just got news that a team caught Rosa at the airport and delivered Melina to a couple. The FBI is swarming around there like bees, they're taking over the investigation."

"We were keeping this quiet until we could get Sam in for questioning. She's going to jeopardize this whole damn thing!"

"What about the Nanny?" Jake asked. "She charged forward and they took her out at the airport."

Lil J picked up his walkie, placing an APB on Mattie McGraw. "Just when she's about to get her life back, she picks the worst time to go nuts and does this to me. I've put my ass on the line for this girl."

"Wait a minute, you didn't see the look on her face." "In a week, she lost her husband, her baby, and her name." "Her life was turned upside down and the one person she trusted more than anything tried to have her knocked off!" "That's not something to get over that fast." "With Mattie, you don't get over it, you get even, in her mind."

"It's too early to go to the campaign headquarters, voters are still at the polls." "Let me go get her and bring her in!" "I have some idea where she might be."

"Fine you have two hours to bring her in, that's all I can spare you."

"Don't worry, I'll get her in time and clean this mess up. Jake hoped he wasn't making promises he couldn't keep.

Mattie took a detour to the campaign headquarters. Just a few hours till the polls would be closed. She knew he wouldn't be there anyway. She drove to the cemetery instead. Out of all the victims in this whole ordeal, her husband was barely mentioned. His family were the only people at the funeral. No friends from the law firm, no one from Mattie's family. Ben's family were aloof, reserved and quiet about their feelings. They had no comments for the reporters. Mattie couldn't believe Ben had turned out so well. He was funny, caring, sweet, and compassionate. Nothing at all like his strange family.

She hated the Sunday dinners with them, his mother was so cold and robotic like. She was quick to point out what was wrong with the house, her decorations, and how she was a lousy cook. His father was patronizing, with a sweet smile and quick to look away with her hurtful comments.

Mattie wanted to pay her last respects for her deceased husband. She drove around the deserted place looking for a newly dug grave, until she found it. She got out of the car, walked towards the site with her stomach turning. The whole place felt eerie and unnerving. "My darling, I can't believe this is the last place I thought I would be." Tears strolled down her cheek, but she didn't lose her composure. She held strong and talked to him as if he could hear every word.

"We've had the most wonderful life together, the both of us." "You made me so happy, the best damn mambo dancer I've ever seen." "I'm sorry your life ended abruptly." "Jake and I took care of your killer though." "He can't harm anyone else ever again." "I'm going to face the true monster now." "I don't know if I can do this, I'm sure as hell going to try, I just miss you, and I want to go home to hear your voice again." She paused, barely getting out the last part, "I'm going to spend my life missing you so much."

She clasped the beautiful jade pendant Ben gave her from all those years ago when they first started dating. She carefully removed it from her neck, kissed it, and placed it on his tombstone. "I can't wear this without you here. I'll always love you, but now I have to go."

She walked away somberly looking for any signs of the police following her, but it was just her there. Passing the enormous statues, hairs on the back of her neck stood up, spooked by their appearance in the dark of night. She knew she would never see Ben again, only in the recesses of her memories he left her with. Melina was still out there and she needed to be brought home. She vowed to never stop looking for her daughter, no matter what the costs.

She was determined to get the Governor any which way possible, even though the entire Police force was searching for her. "He took my life away, now I'm going to return the favor," she thought.

Sam received news of Nanny Rosa's death at the airport. Lenny, his campaign manager and best friend was concerned at how the news would affect his running in the election. He reassured him he would hold a press conference to clear up the details. Sam was frightened, but not willing to quit no matter how terrible things were looking for him. He pursued onwards with the press conference in Louisville, to save face.

"I'm shocked by the news of Rosa's death, as well as the kidnapping of Melina McGraw." His words were well rehearsed, as he continued. This better be good, he thought or my ass is grass. At times during the speech, the Governor trembled, but the words poured out magically to his surprise.

"Let me emphasize that I had no recollection of Rosa's involvement with the small child. I sent her out on an errand run a few days ago to pick up work from Ms. McGraw's house in preparation for my campaign. She was most eager to help me running errands when I needed her. I considered her a good friend and employee as well. It's now apparent that she was one of

the first eye witnesses to discover Ben and Melina McGraw. If I know Rosa as well as I do, she felt sorry for the child and in her own disturbed mind was rescuing that child from Mattie.

Next, he continued the lies, shocking reporters with this next bit of information.

"I've talked with Attorney General McCarthy and have assured them my innocence and gave them my full cooperation. Had I known of Rosa's discrepancies, I would have turned her in myself. I don't believe in vigilantes, I am a great fan of the law and abiding by them too. I am no better than anyone else here today. I believe laws were made to be followed and without them we cannot have a functioning society. As you may know I've been busy campaigning to be your Governor again. You're probably wondering how I couldn't have known Melina was on the premises. As I formally mentioned, I was busy travelling doing work for my campaign. Ask my manager, he will back me up on this issue. They know the truth and now so do you. I ask myself what could I have done to prevent this from happening to Melina. I too have been deceived by two people that I thought I trusted. I have full confidence whomever has this little girl will be tracked down and brought back to her home here in Kentucky. I know that we will bring justice for Ben McGraw and celebrate Melina's safe return. In the last few days, we the people have come to care for this beautiful little girl. She has touched us all with our hearts, especially those fellow parents out there, which I am for certain will hold their own children a little closer and dearer to them.

I urge all parents to keep a closer eye on their children and to have up to date photos of them. We must do everything we can to protect the future generations of this great state. They are our most precious gifts and the future of our greater world."

Things were so quiet among his audience, they stood still bedazzled by his every word, hanging onto every word as if it were their last breath. He assured them that Mattie McGraw would be caught soon and brought to justice for all the pain and suffering he made them believe she caused. Justice would be brought to both the McGraw's and the Jenkins, another piece to the game he was playing.

Wrapping up his speech was risky with new business, but he was a risk taker and felt he was finally in control of his emotions. No more shaking, in fact, he was alive, excited to be there. This was the thing he did best, playing with people's emotions, making bad situations turn into good ones for his own prosperity. He was the master manipulator to a crowd of unsuspecting people. He gave great accolades to the State Police as if they had been buddies their whole life. He said he had great faith in the police, like he was the town sheriff and ready to go bring in a few rustlers.

No more beating around the bush. Sam just got right down to what he thought he wanted to say. "I also believe that it's time to move forward and look to the future ahead of us. I want you to know that I care about the people of this great commonwealth, very much you are all near and dear to my heart." Sam could pour it on like A-1 on a fine steak. "I also promise whatever your decision is today, whether to reelect me or not, I have felt delightful to be your Governor." He began to choke up at his own words again, "God bless you all," he set finishing his speech. His press secretary took over and answered questions one by one. What was his role in all of this and how does he feel about Mattie now? The Governor and his press secretary finished the press conference and a white limousine pulled up.

He impatiently grabbed the phone from her hands, "Give it to me, I'll do it myself right now." They were both interrupted by the ringing of his cell phone. He grasped it tightly and held it close to his ear, hoping anxiously, waiting news from his campaign manager on the voter's returns. The voice on the other end was chilling. "Momma… momma…" "Hello, who is this, who is this" he demanded. "You don't recognize the voice, Governor?" "Mattie, I thought…you were dead." He tried to remain calm, but he was terrorized, so scared he wanted to jump out of his skin. "That's a good one Sam. After I get through with you, you're gonna wish I was dead. The suicide note was really convincing too. You always did have a way with words."

"Mattie, you should turn yourself in, I'm sure we can help you." Her laughs were high pitched and drove chills through his heart. "I just visited with my dead husband, he sends his regards." You took Ben, you took my daughter, now I'm going to take everything you care about away." The governor paused, frightened. "Please Mattie", barely plausible and there was dead silence. He panicked momentarily. Scollini had to be dead if she's still alive. His plans were falling apart at the seams. "Oh my God," he blurted out. "It was Mattie McGraw."

He took a deep breath and tried to get ahold of his emotions to keep from having a major meltdown. He called Lil J and told him about the disturbing phone call and how it upset him. Lil J had a smirk on his face. He tried to calm him down and suggested meeting with him at a secret location. They agreed to meet outside at an old abandoned warehouse in Frankfort. Sam was hesitant at first, but agreed reluctantly. He was still upset that Mattie took off, but he loved the fact that she shook his tree and all the leaves were falling off. He decided it was his mission to take Sam down and restore truth and honesty.

CHAPTER 11

The couple that took Melina at the airport was identified. The news was worldwide. Victor Schwartz sat glued to the television watching the biography splashed across the screen. Fifty-two-year-old Victor Schwartz and his forty-seven year old wife Georgianna came from old money. Together their riches were estimated at almost forty billion dollars. They almost lost it all when the IRS found out they hadn't paid taxes since they were married. Victor was powerful with lots of riches, powerful friends, including friends in the IRS. A deal was made it was decided that they would pay back taxes but only half of what they were supposed to pay. After that, they moved.

Victor was smart and conniving and he knew how to take care of money matters, but this kidnapping thing was way over his head. Melina had to disappear, like it never happened. Victor met his wife at the end of the stairs. Georgianna begged to keep her but her pleas were useless. He placed his hand on her teary-eyed face, "I'm sorry, but this was all a mistake." "We can't keep her." "We're not spending the rest of our lives in jail for kidnapping." "She has to go back." Georgianna had already attached herself to Melina. She loved playing with her and singing to her as she was her own child. She fought hard to keep her, but she did was she was always told.

She knew it was useless. Victor always won the debates or confrontations. He was demanding and stubborn and she was sweet and demure. "I'm sorry sweetheart, but the governor sold us a river that doesn't exist." "We are innocent, we didn't know that she was taken from Kentucky and there was a murder involved."

She agreed to fetch her and bring her to him. "What will you do with her?" A stream of tears was rolling down her face. "You won't hurt her promise me that!" "Hun, I'm not a monster, she's just a baby." But what Victor had in mind for her was far worse than his dutiful wife could ever imagine. "Why can't we just go to the police and explain this whole thing?" "Do you honestly think they will believe anything we say at this point?" "No, they'll take our asses into jail for kidnapping." "Don't worry darling, I will take care of everything." "When the time is right, we'll adopt a baby, the right way." She couldn't even imagine his dark side. He concocted a plan to rid themselves of the sparkly little baby with rolls around her arms, legs and little cheeks. A trip out of the country was what they needed and after a while she would forget about the baby completely.

First, he had to take care of the overzealous and clingy wife. He knew just how to do that. He procured a bottle of valium and dropped in two tablets into a hot cup of tea. He walked slowly to the upstairs nursery and placed the cup of tea carefully on the dresser. "Hun, I brought you something to help you settle your nerves and help you sleep." He placed his hand on her shoulder. She couldn't face him. She couldn't show him her hurt and pain looming. Melina felt like a death in her small family. Having a chance to be a mother and having it taken away so suddenly was more than she could fathom. Victor seemed so cold and nonchalant about losing the baby. After all she thought, she was supposed to be his daughter too. He could sense that she was heartbroken. "We can't keep her. She already has a family in Kentucky." She didn't respond to him at first. He grabbed her and turned her around slowly. "Look at me darling." His voice grew softer and sympathetic. She could barely muster a nod with her head. "I love you sweetheart." "Don't worry about Melina, she'll be fine. I'll get you another child, one that cannot be taken away." Grasping her hand tightly to comfort her, I promise from the bottom of my heart I will make this up to you." Tears welled up in her eyes. She began to shake uncontrollably and began sobbing. "Say goodbye to her now." She couldn't bring herself to wake Melina up. She bent down and gently kissed her rosy cheeks.

Melina seemed peaceful and content. "She looks like an angel sleeping." He couldn't bring himself to share this tender moment with her. He had to keep a clear head if this little problem was going to go away. She had to fight the urge to leave her because she knew this would be the last time she would ever see her again. She wanted this picture of the baby to stay etched in her memory forever.

"What are you going to do with her? I have a right to know," she demanded. Victor searched for the answers fast, the right ones that would appease his heartbroken wife. "As soon as you go to sleep I will take her and turn her over to the authorities. From there, they can send her back where she belongs."

"Are we going to jail," she worriedly asked.

"No, I'll explain everything, we didn't know she was kidnapped and that we had no recollection of this. I'll bring our lawyers with me and he'll explain and make them understand our point of view. Georgianna, we were victims too."

"Well yes, we were lied to."

"That's right, we were made pawns in this whole ordeal."

He thought, "Good, she's finally coming back to her senses." He grabbed her face, pulling her close to him. He gently kissed her quivering lips. "Drink this tea I brought you and you'll feel much better. She let out a huge sigh. There was no fighting Victor, his will to win was too strong and her willpower was shattered into thousands of little shards. Broken heart, broken spirit. She sipped the tea and sat down in the creaky rocking chair, staring at the baby who would be halfway across the country. Everything slowly became a blur, she couldn't fight the urge to stay awake. Her tired, overwhelming body wouldn't allow her to.

Victor came from behind, leans over and whispered into her ear, "I love you darling. When you awake in the morning we'll be long gone from here and have a new life waiting for us." He gently picked his tired wife, putting her to her bed, lovingly placing her under the silk sheets that the best money could afford. She was unconscious, almost comatose in her state. He swept the hair from her face and stroked her cheek. He was relieved, now onto important matters. Time was crucial, the police would be there shortly. He sees that Melina was tuckered out too.

He picked up the snoozing baby, grabbing the blanket in the crib. He placed her in the car seat with the price tag still attached. He fastened her in, with her head drooping to the side as she remained in a dreamlike state. He ran to the driver's side of his car, hits the gas and floors it from the driveway. Little did he know that the police were already surveilling them from afar. They were waiting for the moment to make their move on the Schwartz house and rescue the baby. Victor headed over to the bridge down by the river. Roads were curvy, but that didn't stop him from driving like a maniac. The fog gave way to an eerier, darker night. He went over the plan in his head over and over.

Step 1: Throw Melina over the bridge
Step 2: Run back to the house.
Step 3: Retrieve Georgianna
Step 4: Finally leave this madness behind them.

No baby meant no proof of kidnapping which would ultimately mean no arrest to be made. "There's no way in hell they'll pin this on us," he thought. "If by some chance they catch us, we'll stick to the story, we never had her in the first place."

He had no ill-will towards Melina, he liked her in the way a father loved his children. She was well behaved, intelligent than most infants her age, and for that he felt remorseful.

Twenty minutes passed as Victor frantically drove to Melina's final destination. In the car seat she slept peacefully, cooing with a tiny smile on her face. He looked around cautiously for anyone or anything that could interfere with his foolproof plan. He nervously fidgeted with the seat belt and unfastening the car seat from the car. He yanked her out of the car, pulling her closely to his chest. The fog made for difficulty to cover the acts that were about to take place. With no one in sight, he tiptoed away from the car, to keep the sleeping baby at peace. His guilt was overbearing, how could he take away this innocent child's life and how could he face his teary-eyed wife's face? These questions clouded his mind. "Never mind," he thought. "This is a problem, and I'm a problem solver," he tried to think with clarity. "She has to go, tonight." He reached for the trash bag in his front seat, and continued to walk towards the middle of the creaking bridge.

His heart raced, holding her tightly to his chest. This would be a mercy killing, he rationalized. She would feel no pain, and this nightmare would be over once and for all. Once more, he looked around his surroundings, making sure there were no witnesses. The fog grew heavily, making out things uneasily. Much like an apparition Georgianna appeared out of the night with her white night gown flowing in the wind. He thought this was all an illusion, induced by stress. "This can't be happening," he thought. He stood frozen in place as she inched closer to him. "Where did you come from," he stuttered. "How in the world are you here?" "I am here," she responded as she extended out her arm.

"But what about the…" "What, the valium you decided to put in my tea?" she cut him off. "I switched that earlier in the day. For you see I've known you long enough to know that's exactly the kind of stunt you would pull. I'm not as stupid as you think I am. She continued telling how she knew and how she set him up.

"I heard you earlier on the phone, making our supposed getaway plans and the call to the pharmacist. I then switched the labels on you when you weren't looking replacing the valium for vitamin C pills.

Victor was stunned. "How could you betray me like that?"

"Hurts doesn't it," she retorted. The screams startled Melina as she became alert of everything. "It's over Victor, hand her over."

"But what about us? The life we had planned together?"

"You were going to murder this innocent child, and for what… a jail free card? Did you really think I would be with a heartless monster like you? I see you for what you truly are."

She snatched the baby from his grasps. Victor dropped to his knees, "Please baby… I just wanted our life the way it was before." She spat, "You had the opportunity to do the right thing, but instead you thought of only yourself, and wanted to kill a baby."

Out from the foggy view stepped in a police force, surrounding them and ready to intervene. The tall rookie officer read him his rights as he handcuffed Victor, as they both stepped off into the eerie night, back to his vehicle. Georgianna kissed Melina on her forehead, handing her over to the authorities. "Excellent job, Mrs. Schwartz," an investigator said. She knew she was doing what was best for the little baby she got to know.

It was earlier that day that she was contacted by the FBI while she was out shopping and convinced her to help in the investigation. Everything in her heart knew that her husband was acting suspicious with the cagey phone calls, and being cryptic with the dealings. The police wanted Victor to think he could come and go as he pleased, only to step in at the right time. There were over one hundred operatives surrounding the bridge at that moment. She felt safe being surrounded by so many guns aimed at Victor.

CHAPTER 12

$\mathcal{M}$attie rushed to the car, reflecting on everything that had blasted her life to pieces starting with the gruesome images she wished she never saw. It worsened as she thought of her ransacked house, which was once filled with happy memories only replaced by the shock of finding her deceased husband on the floor. Watching her daughter being driven off by a crazed woman in a red coat, these thoughts, flooded like a slow-motion picture. "This is where I am now," she thought. "Not another moment to waste." She had to shrug these memories from her mind, staying focused on her current revengeful mission.

She yearned to hold her daughter once more, but she had a cold-heartless bastard to deal with. The adrenaline coursed through her veins, never feeling this alive before. No one was going to deter her from this vendetta this time. She knew Lil J and Jake meant well, but they couldn't possibly understand the position she was in, anguish and exhaustion. She took in a deep breath, started the engine, unaware of what would happen next.

Her revengeful game would have to wait as she saw a dark figure in the fog. She whipped to the dark seat, locked the doors and hid from view. She was afraid to speak or move so little as an inch. This was the angriest she had ever seen Jake. He was usually smiling and had this laid back attitude on life. This time was an exception, livid he was, red in the face with crazy bulging eyes. Her eyes looked pitiful, full of remorse, truly sorry for the acts she had done.

"You always speak before you think, don't you Mattie? You act before you take the time to realize what the consequences will be," he lectured. "Not this time, Mattie," he said slowly moving his finger from her lips. She opened her mouth to start speaking. "Nope, this time you listen to me. You could've jeopardized this whole operation with your carelessness. You could've screwed everything up with the Governor! Lil J and the entire Kentucky State Police are working together to bring him down. They are so close to getting him and returning your daughter back. You need to trust us that we're doing the right thing here!" He placed his strong hands around her tiny shoulders wanting to shake her, but couldn't bring himself to do it. He leaned into her with ferocious eyes. "I get where you're coming from, really I do, but for once can you let someone help you through this?" For the first time, she wanted to turn all of her problems over to someone else. Almost completely. Mattie was on a mission to clear her name and to get her daughter back. Leaving this up to the men was not her style at all. In a way, she felt like Rambo, shoot now, ask the questions never. All she could think about was Melina was out there somewhere. She felt tormented worrying if she was being taken care of. Is she warm enough, is she being fed, is she asking for me, she wondered.

Jake and Lil J had been good to her so far, and she felt like she had no choice but to seek their help, her hands were tied. She had to follow their instructions, their ways, their plans. She longed for Ben to be there, to guide her through. He was always the level headed one. He always had a plan, a solution for anything. She was mesmerized by his forcefulness and his authoritativeness. He knew she had a temper and reasoning with her was useless when her mind was made up, but sometimes it led her to trouble. He was calm and reasonable, sometimes she hated to admit it but he was usually right.

She snapped back to herself, "I guess I have no choice, but to ask for your help. I'm sorry I ran off causing you trouble Jake. Whatever your plan is, count me in."

Meanwhile at the Jenkin's Manor, Nicole couldn't understand what bothered her more. That slimy snake was going to be reelected as Kentucky's Governor. Maybe it was the fact that an innocent woman was paying for her sins, as horrid as they were. Death all around, kidnappings, and missing, she wished she had a crystal ball to track

Mattie's whereabouts. "Lord knows where that distressed woman is," she muttered. Where were these feelings coming from, she pondered. Nicole was as stoic as they came when it came to emotions, but she was quite the actress when she had to be. She only allowed herself to feel anything real when she was draped in her lover's arms.

It wasn't that she was robotic, just cautious about wearing her heart on her sleeve and never showing how she felt to an unexpecting public. This was something her dearly deceased husband Seth taught her. Still, she felt bad for Mattie McGraw. Setting her up was payback to her father. That was an evil idea concocted for some time. Having Seth taken out was just a bonus and didn't bother her much. In fact, she even chuckled in her sleep, because to her Seth was useless.

She liked to imagine the terrified look on his face when he was pleading his life to Scollini. She even slept with Scollini once just to get back at him for ignoring her need to be loved. It was a scary one-night stand in a cheap motel out of the way. Seth was meeting one of his political advisors and she was just bored. She loved looking at Scollini at his sculpted physique. He reminded her of her current lover, only Scollini had sociopathic tendencies. He was built like a Greek god, gorgeous, jet black hair, curled, and olive skin that added to his impressive complexion. She fantasized of running her fingertips through his luscious thick hair and touching his smooth, sculpted curvaceous body. He was a sexy object that made her heart flutter. From the first encounters, she stepped into the room, Scollini was in control. His breathy deep voice chilled and excited her, unknowing of what to expect.

"Come here kitten," he snarled as he grabbed her by the back of her neck, slamming her into the wall. She almost lost her balance and was left breathless. He rubbed her neck and slammed her face into his, pressing her bloody engorged lips hard, and tightly squeezing her hips. Before she could react, Scollini ripped off her dress and threw it across the room. He fashioned a mischievous grin on his face. His dark eyes rolled with delight like a great white shark that caught his prey. It was the game Scollini loved playing, terrorizing his new toys.

Nicole thought she was going to die that night. Her body ached with fear after the flashback passed through her mind. She was usually fearless, confident, and not easily swayed, however when he was through with her, she was left on the floor wrecked. She was left cold, naked and disorientated from the events of that night. Her body battered, bruised, bloody, and her face disfigured and unrecognizable, even when she managed to look at her reflection. His hatred towards women penetrated her body and she was terrified of him.

She was grateful when it was over. Scollini laughed hysterically at the hypocrisy of it all. She wanted him, she needed him. Scollini needed no one. He got great satisfaction of playing with his toys, over and over. Women were useless and he let them know it. He was relentless with her and he informed her when he was done with her. Her eyes glazed with fear. Nicole endured three long hours of terror, torment, and being brutalized by Scollini. "Just keep your damn mouth shut, or I'll finish you and your husband off!" "Understand?" She nodded haphazardly. She understood. He made a quick exit, and she relieved a long drawn out sigh of relief. She was his prisoner for hours, and suffered at his hands, but she could live another day.

He was one intimidating S.O.B that shook up Nicole, as she became leerier of men after that. She vowed never to let a man control her or allow herself to be beaten brutally like a dog. She was enraged reliving that atrocious night with him. She momentarily had forgotten where she was being wrapped up in an aura of tormenting terror. She vaguely remembered clasping a wine glass filled with the finest Merlot, clasping too tightly to where the shards of glass cut her blood dripping hand. This wave of pain brought her out of her terror visions. She leapt into the kitchen, quickly grabbing a white terrycloth towel to control the searing pain and blood cascading down her hand like a fountain.

Her body trembled as tears poured out hard and fast. She wasn't used to all these emotions pouring out at once. According to Seth, crying was useless. It felt good to be almost human-like for once. Nicole hugged herself, taking long labored breaths. She was in control now, something she liked. This made her life less complicated. She daydreamed of better things, such as taking over Seth's seat and sending Sam to the big house, begging for mercy. In all this, she was remorseful for Mattie, but she was paying for the father's sins. Nicole couldn't care less for politics, but revenge on Sam and Mattie was a dish best served chilled with her long vengeful hands.

Nicole decided to keep quiet with her plans until the right moment. She still owned pictures of Seth's killing and decided to turn them over to the police very soon. She knew she was taking a huge chance of being caught, but she didn't care. There was no money or contract exchanged. She was still angry about Scollini and the Governor needed to pay. After all, Scollini was his hit man and she decided Sam would be the next target.

Kentuckians were mowing each other over to cast their vote for Sam. News reports predicted a landslide victory for Sam. People were excited about the election even though there was no one else running against him. He built up so much momentum about women's rights and protection for the children that teacher unions were backing his nomination. The people were moved by his speech and had adopted Melina as their own. The people used this example to keep a better watch on their own children.

The Lexington residents weren't as optimistic, with their attitudes shifting after the events of the McGraw family. They were scared to keep their doors unlocked at night. Everyone became fearful and paranoid of break-ins and burglaries. Gun sales skyrocketed and people weren't as trusting anymore. Overnight, it was as if the people of Lexington vanished from the streets. What was once a beautiful, scenic paradise became a ghost town. People simply went to work and then came home to their families.

They watched their kids ever so closely and their babies even closer. Fear permeated the air in Lexington and the people were preparing for the worst to come. It was as though Armageddon itself had reared its ugly head. What was once a kind, open, safe community of smiling, trusting people changed. It became quickly replaced with suspicious, grimaced, protective soldiers ready for battle. The mood of the community was fearful and angry. With the last presidential election, it brought a slew of angry and embittered women everywhere. These were the people hoping to see their first woman president, reflecting that the times were changing.

That wasn't to be however, the younger generation stole the election. Blamed for their endless apathy towards politics and voting, they stepped up to the plate this time. They were sly and smart, using their resources on the Internet to swing millions of votes for their prospective candidate. He was perceived as a real winner by most. He was smart, good-looking, confident and articulate to the tee. No one knew much about him or anything in his background, but his campaign jubilated excitement and people were ready to follow their leader like a prophet who claims to perform miracles. The Democratic party was divided, in more ways than one.

Millions of women were ready to cross party lines and vote for their female candidate. People weren't happy with the choices. Either vote for the tall cool inexperienced one or the clueless one who just wanted the title and had no real plans for change. Revenge at the polls were on the voters' devious minds. People were screaming for change everywhere, but change terrified them as well from both sides of the political spectrum. People were afraid to make the wrong choice again.

The economy was hit hard by foreclosures, the stock market, war, and inflation from the food and gas prices. People were desperate for new solutions to old problems and counting down the days to the presidential election.

Lil J finally got the call he longed for. The FBI called with the news about Melina. She was retrieved from Mrs. Schwartz. He was mortified from the details and for the safety of the baby. Luckily Mattie was nowhere to be found to hear the story of Mr. Schwartz's plan to dispose of her little girl.

"The rescue went smoothly," said a voice over the phone. "Things are looking good on our end, but the Governor hasn't been arrested yet," replied Lil J. "We've discussed meeting at a secret location."

"Nooooo!" Lil J said. "Cancel it, we're grabbing him here at the mansion."

"It'll have to wait until the election is over. We have to get this girl back first." "The Lieutenant Governor is waiting in the wings to take over as soon as possible." "We're waiting till Sam is arrested." "What about Mattie, you realize she's innocent." "Yeah, we're aware of this." "forensics took another sweep through the house, We've, matched hair follicles to that rogue cop Scollini." "You've got the girl right?" Lil J hated lying to the FBI and knew this could ultimately cost him his job for good, if he was found out that is.

"Jake Diamond, a private investigator I've been working with has found her and is bringing her in as we speak." "Good, very good." The agent seemed pleased. "Looks like we're going to have quite the mother-daughter reunion after all. I'll let you know the rest of the details later, until then keep this matter quiet. No press either!"

Jake had good instincts. His great hunt for Mattie finally paid off. He was really moved by Mattie saying goodbye to Ben at the cemetery. He was moved by the sentiment of it all. He was relieved Mattie was in control of her own emotions. He practically threatened her to take a nap on the drive back to the mansion. "Those fuzzy handcuffs really came in handy," he thought.

She was cuffed to the door handle, she wasn't going off anywhere, he chuckled. Jake loved watching her sleep, enjoying the peaceful and serene look on her face. It gave him hope for her and getting back her life. Maybe, just maybe Mattie McGraw was going to be ok. Someday soon. Normally, he was apathetic toward his clients, but not with her.

She had his number and he knew it. Beaver Dam High ran through his brain. He fell in love with her and the first moment he laid eyes upon her. They made searing, passionate love. It wasn't something meaningless like all of the other one-night stands. It started out very slowly and gentle at first. He gently caressed her small round face. Her eyes were very deep and endearing. Her skin was soft and her legs were long and then like a ballet dancer.

Jake looked sexier than ever. Mattie was completely into him and completely turned on. That night at the football stadium was magic for both. He wore a white rugby t-shirt and tight blue jeans revealing his firm buttocks.

Before she could catch her breath, Jake pulled out a picnic basket, "I thought we could have some wine and strawberries."

Jake held out his hand and led her to the middle of the football field. They laid out on a red-checkered blanket. Jake poured Mattie a glass as he smiled at her coyly.

"Is this your first time Mattie?" Jake questioned.

She almost choked on her first sip and dropped her glass.

"I mean to drink wine?"

She breathed a sigh of relief.

"Oh…well, yeah," she replied, "I guess you drink it all the time."

"No, only on special occasions with a special girl," he said.

"Actually," Jake confessed, "I borrowed it from my mother's special collection."

Mattie and Jake talked and laughed for hours. They both were entranced with each other. Jake leaned over and slowly placed his hand on the nape of her neck, slowly pulling her into him.

They kissed for a moment. The longer they kissed, the more carried away they became with each other. Mattie slowly laid back on the blanket. Her heart was scurrying, she felt breathless, but in a good way.

CHAPTER 13

Sam never felt more confident and excited in his life. The election would soon be his. Madeline McGraw would soon be in jail and all this craziness would be behind him. He knew what was best for Kentucky and they were embracing him with open arms of trust, love, and affection. He was caught up for a moment in his victory to come and the outstanding speech he had planned to give. He pictured himself standing at the podium with echoes of "I am Sam, I can do anything you think I can!" The audience was screaming, Sam, Sam, Sam. His cell phone brought him back to reality for the moment.

"Hello, who is this?" He bellowed. "Sam this is Lenny."

"You're not going to like this. "So just listen to me, ok." Why Lenny, nothing you can say today is going to get my goat." "Didn't you hear?" "I'm winning by a landslide!" "Unless you want to conjure up a dead man for debate." "Ha! Ha!" "Sam knock it off!" "This is serious!" "Turn on your tv!" "I don't have time for this!" "Nonsense!" "Sam just turn on the television now!" It was loud at his headquarters, phones ringing off the hook, people were running around everywhere. He quietly walked into his office and shut the door abruptly and locked it.

For privacy, he pulled the blinds behind him and switched to his favorite news station. The news reporter was his favorite too.

She had interviewed him many times before. He was very attracted to her intriguing smile and wavy blonde hair. Plus, she was assertive and not afraid to ask the hard questions. Julie Welch was respected by everyone and when she spoke, people paid attention. Sam couldn't believe what he was hearing. It came spilling out of her mouth like venom.

His smile turned to fear and panic surrounded him. "The people of Kentucky have a lot to celebrate today." "The much anticipated return of Melina McGraw." "Authorities in Switzerland have confirmed the baby was rescued earlier in Switzerland." "Apparently, Georgianna and Victor Swartz paid fifty-thousand dollars to adopt the child." "According to police, Mr. Swartz also attempted to kill the small child by throwing her over a bridge to drown her, but police thwarted his attempts and arrested him on site."

"His wife is not currently being charged and is being praised by police as an advocate that helped to save Melina's life." "Victor Swartz is currently in jail on charges of attempted murder and kidnapping. "Sam, Sam it's over Sam!" "If they connect you with the nanny and Mattie it's over!" Sam's face was red, furious with anger that Scollini hadn't finished the job he was paid very well to do.

He wanted to be the Governor of Kentucky again more than anything, but his lies, betrayal, and plots were finally catching up with him. "I'm waiting outside for you!" "The jet is gassed up and ready to go!" He knew if he stayed in Kentucky his life would be over. He would lose his freedom and go to jail. He never imagined it would end like this. But Sam always had a plan. He had Swiss bank accounts and houses in Paris, Italy, Greece, and Ireland. Having a millionaire for a best friend didn't hurt either. "Sam talk to me, I'm trying to save your life as we know it!" "I'm on my way out!" He opened the door to cheers and campaign volunteers who rushed to him and surrounded him.

He pushed his way through the crowd of smiles and congratulations and ran out the door not looking back. He was relieved at the sight of Lenny's black Mercedes and jumped in for the great escape of his life. He dove into the passenger seat with his feet up in the air and Lenny hit the gas. They raced toward the airport like two Nascar drivers ready for speed and lots of crazy curves and bumps along the way.

Sam had lost it literally. He was shaking and weeping and babbling and not making any sense. Lenny hated to see his best friend fall apart. He wasn't too good with crying and emotions. "Listen to me Sam, everything is going to be ok." "Haven't I always got your back?" Sam was blubbering and crying and nodding at the same time.

He was overwhelmed with the fear of getting caught and sent to prison. He cried all the way to the airport, while Lenny tried his best to calm him down and set him straight. "Where are we going?" Sam said calmly. Sam finally got a hold of his crying and his nerves and stopped shaking. "Why Mr. Sam we are off to the land of fine wines, warm beer, and where people know to keep their mouths shut." "What if the FBI are already following us?" "No problem, my plane has an anti-tracking device and a fixed flight plan that we won't be taking my friend.

"I've done some very bad things Lenny." "Sam, we all make mistakes." "Maybe I deserve to go to jail and pay for every bad thing I've done." "Stop it Sam!" "You've also done many good things too!" "When you were Governor of Kentucky you brought about all those women's programs that actually saved abused women." "You brought hundreds, not one or two, but hundreds of jobs to unemployed people, who would still be sitting at home." "You made some mistakes, yes that's true, but you performed so many good deeds. "I'm not going to let you beat yourself up anymore." "Sam, you were an amazing Governor and that's part of your legacy forever!"

"Sam, you have a life time to pay your retribution and to do good deeds!" "Everything that's messed up in Kentucky will settle itself." "You're sixty-five years old!" "You wouldn't make it a week in prison." "I'm giving you a future!" "It's not time to pay back for all the stupid things you've done!" "I'm offering you a life with no prison walls and prison guards to tell you when to wake up and when to go to sleep." "Man, I'm offering you freedom, so take it whether you think you deserve it or not!" "Do you hear me!" Sam nodded, this was his only chance to live a free life.

Maybe someday he could help Mattie McGraw and atone for Ben's murder and kidnapping Melina. Right now, he just wanted to save himself. They boarded the small plane quickly and Lenny screamed orders to the captain. They took off headed toward the eastern seaboard. The flight plan was for California. However, as soon as they flew over the Atlantic ocean, they changed flight plans immediately.

They changed direction falling off the radar and heading toward France. Lenny was smart about everything, including no extradition.

There was no extradition from Nice, France. Sam could live his life freely and walk amongst the crowds without having to look over his back. They toasted.

"Here's to new adventures in our new life." "As far as Kentucky is concerned, they're getting the dumbest Lt. Governor to ever hold an office." "So long suckers!" This made Sam laugh hysterically and they clinked glasses.

"Lil'J apparently Governor Sam got hold of the news Melina was being brought back to Kentucky and bolted from his campaign headquarters with his best friend Lenny." "They took off for California and in the middle of the Atlantic, dropped off the radar." "The tower couldn't pick it up!"

"We've got teams searching for them as we speak!" "Of all the stupid things I've heard!" "You all really screwed this one up!" Each FBI agent in the room held their face down. Agent Darryl Martin wasn't taking the blame for this one. He spoke blatantly. "You know what I don't need right now is attitude from some hick in the boonies!" Lil'J responded with assurance. "Sir, I say this with the deepest felt sympathies!" "Kiss my ass!" "Here's what I want!" "We need to clean this up fast!" "I want the baby brought to the Governor's mansion, as soon as she arrives."

"I want the Lt. Governor informed of what is going on and to hold a press conference in the next hour!" "No more, no less!" "You can't make demands on me!" "Just shut-up and listen!" "This is my area and I'll run it however I damn well please!" "I also want all charges against Mattie McGraw cleared immediately!" "Do we understand each other?" "Yes sir!" agent Martin retorted angrily.

Lt. Governor Stone Maupin was informed of the Governor's quick exit from Kentucky. He didn't take it so well. Stone was used to following orders, not giving them. There was nothing extraordinary about Stone Maupin. He was completely anxiety ridden. Stone feared the people were going to be angry about Sam lying to them and their families. He was petrified. This evening he would step into the Governor's position, with much shame over his party's head. There would be no victory party.

"I hope the smarmy bastard gets caught!" he whispered to himself. He never liked him anyway. Tonight, there would be a very quiet swearing in and a news conference. Stone was an excellent speaker and wrote most of Sam's speeches. His first plan of action was to start an investigation into the Governor's whereabouts and to clear Mattie McGraw of all the charges against her. He wasn't cold-hearted like Sam, he felt truly mortified for Mattie after her was informed of Scollini's attempts on Jake and Mattie's lives. He knew she was suffering greatly because of Sam. Stone wanted to make things right for Mattie and the people of Kentucky.

Jake and Mattie finally reached the mansion. Jake was following orders to bring her back to the police. His instinct told him to gun it and get out of there as quick as possible. But he trusted Lil'J. Police cars were lined up from the entrance to the outside. They were given the ok to go through the gate.

Every news station surrounded them. Reporters were in a frenzy, chasing every car in sight. Jake and Mattie were unrecognizable still dressed in their new costumes. The sirens and police cars woke Mattie up. "We're here, darling!" Jake announced hesitantly. "We're back at the mansion." "It's time to wake up." "What's going on Jake?"

"I don't know Mattie." "My gut tells me either Sam has been arrested or he's fled." "Stupid FBI, they could have ended this before there was even an election." "I'm scared Jake." He grabbed her for reassurance and squeezed her tightly. "You'll go and tell them your story Mattie." "Tell them how Sam set you up for Seth's murder, killed Ben, and took Melina." "You've got me and Lil'J on your side." "It's time to stop running darling!" "I promise I'll do whatever I can to help you." "We're the good guys remember?" "And the good guys always win." Jake looked at Mattie with open eyes. He felt so proud to be by her side at this moment.

They had remained friends for a long time, but he felt so close to this woman. He loved everything about her. Her small, round face glowed when she smiled. Her deep green eyes seemed effervescent and soft. She was truly the most neurotic, stressful, loud and opinionated woman he had ever met or known. He knew he was going to have to give her up for awhile and that really hurt. He knew deep in his heart they would be together again someday.

As they flew up the stairs to the Governor's office, Mattie stopped dead in her tracks and gazed at her friend. Plus, she was very emotional and so tired of running. "Words cannot express how much I appreciate you being there for me." She looked extremely tired and her eyes were hazy, but she was also starched with adrenalin running through her veins. She was ready to take on the world. She let out a deep breath, her eyes were glazed, but she felt no tears.

She had shed many tears for Ben. "I'm going to miss you Jake." He pulled her close to him and he held her gently for a minute. "Come on Mattie, quit stalling." "Lil'J is waiting for us and it's all going to turn out alright." "I promise." Mattie could not understand why Jake was pulling her so adamantly. She felt like the lamb being thrown into the wolve's den.

"Momma……momma… echoed throughout the hall as a big blue ball rolled into the hallway with a little girl chasing it. She stopped dead in her tracks releasing Jake's hand. She put her hand to her heart grinning from ear to ear. She looked at him still confused. She wasn't sure what to do next. Maybe this was a trap and as soon as she came near Melina the FBI would haul her away in handcuffs. Not a scene she wanted her daughter to go through. Or maybe Lil'J and Jake planned this all along.

She wasn't sure what reality was anymore. Maybe she was daydreaming and when she approached Melina she would vanish like everything else had in the past couple of weeks. Jake grabbed Mattie's face softly with trusting eyes. He knew she was hesitant and scared to move forward, even though she wanted to. "It's your daughter Mattie!" He turned and pointed in her direction. "Go be with her, it's really ok!" Melina clenched her fists in her mouth with anticipation and giggled with delight. She knew who mommy was. She held out her hands toward her Mother. Mattie couldn't stand it anymore.

She saw Lil'J step out of the office. He nodded toward her with a boyish aw' shucks kind of grin. "It's ok!" He said reassured. "It's ok to pick her up Mattie." That's all she needed to hear. She tore off in flight running and scooped up Melina in her arms. Melina's eyes lit up instantly.

"Momma…momma she said over and over which were joyous noises to her. She was unaware of the thunderous noises surrounding her.

Lil'J and Jake and the FBI agents were clapping loudly. The whole room was charged with electricity and good vibes. "Congratulations, Mattie!" "You deserve it!" This was the moment she had dreamed about for weeks. She felt part of her tormented soul restored as she clung dearly to her darling little infant.

She pictured Ben smiling profusely down upon them blowing them a kiss from heaven and giving her the nod everything was going to be alright again in her life. She was uneasy by the sight of the agents and began walking slowly toward them ready to face whatever they might throw at her. Lil'J looked at Mattie smiling brightly. "Don't worry Mattie!" he said. "All charges have been dropped, he said excitedly. "They just want to hear your story."

Mattie felt great relief. Like the world had been taken off her shoulders. "That's fine Lil'J, I guess they'll be arresting the Governor now." His face dropped along with the other FBI agents. Jake looked puzzled. "What's going on here?" "Why isn't Sam in custody?" "Oh my God!" "You morons let him escape!" Agent Darryl Martin tried to explain. "The Governor took off this afternoon from his headquarters with his friend Lenny."

"They apparently boarded a small plane for California, but dropped off the radar over the Atlantic." "We have agents all over the world looking for them right now." How could you have let this happen?" Mattie scoffed furiously. "Miss McGraw we had planned on grabbing him at the mansion. However, we believe he received news Melina was found and back on her way to Kentucky."

"Melina would have tied him to the kidnapping and Ben's murder." "We believe he panicked and fled the scene before we could apprehend him." "How did anyone find out Melina was coming home and why wasn't I the first to know about my daughter being found?" She snarled brazenly. "Well we informed Lil'J and we thought he would let you know." "Unless you weren't around to get the news." "The only person to blame is the one I'm looking at right now."

"I'm sorry Miss McGraw, we had to keep things quiet till we received orders to obtain the suspect." Agent Martin was finally without words. He knew he had dropped the ball on this one and Mattie knew it too. He quickly became defensive and was annoyed with her. "Look the Swiss police leaked to reporters about Melina's rescue." Miss McGraw, you must have so many questions about what happened to your daughter." She leered at him blatantly. "Oh, believe me, I do!" He tried to lighten the situation a little. "You have a beautiful girl, Miss McGraw." "She didn't have a scratch on her and she seems to have taken the trip well."

"That's fine, I'm grateful for that." "Thank you for rescuing my little girl." She cooled her heels as she began to filter in all the details. "If you'll come into the office we'll fill you in on your daughter's rescue and we have some questions for you too." "This might take awhile." Mattie searched Darryl's eyes with distress.

"Miss McGraw is there something else on your mind?" "We understand you've been through a lot." "We just need the details of the day you found the pictures and your husband's murder." "Yeah, there is something on my mind." "Chaos in Kentucky." The news was out triple fold. Kentuckians were being blasted with news reports on every channel, from nationwide to local.

Julie Welch delivered the news with a sparkle in her eye breaking the news about Melina. "Melina McGraw, Kentucky's adopted baby of the bluegrass is back in Kentucky after a daring and brave rescue attempt by the FBI and Switzerland's police force." "A reunion between Melina and her mother took place today at the Governor's mansion. "According to the police Mattie McGraw has been cleared of all charges of murdering Seth Jenkins and her husband Ben McGraw." Cheers rang out across Kentucky from houses, to people in bars clicking drinks and singing.

People were ecstatic with the news of Melina coming home where she belonged. As the election results were delivered with Sam's landslide victory, there was breaking news also.

"Governor Sam has disappeared and is nowhere to be found." "According to his campaign volunteers, Sam abruptly left his headquarters this afternoon in a black Mercedes benz." According to our sources, Governor Sam is a person of interest and under investigation for the murder of Seth Jenkins, his one-time opponent." She drew a long, surprised face and continued. "Lt. Governor Stone Maupin is being sworn in now and is set to step in for Governor Sam." "Let's go live to Stone's acceptance speech."

CHAPTER 14

Chaos in Kentucky was erupting everywhere, bubbling up like catechisms and exploding instantaneously. The people of Kentucky were angry about Governor Sam leaving them and lying to them. They were demanding answers fast. Stone Maupin was minutes away from giving the speech of his life outside the Governor's mansion. He knew what he was going to say, but he didn't know if he would pass out or throw up or both.

To be given such a huge responsibility of governing the bluegrass was completely overwhelming to Stone. He felt like a trapped rat wanting to run for the nearest exit. He was shredding to pieces. Everything around him was chaotic. Loud, screaming news reporters placated the mansion. Sam's assistant was now Stone's assistant. She was talking at light speed, but nothing was making sense. He was caught in an aura of jumbled words. He couldn't quite make them out at first. Ms. Cates smiled and touched his hand.

She sensed his uneasiness and hesitancy to take on this huge responsibility. "Stone this is your moment." "You can do this." "You can win them over." "Sam was arrogant and made a huge mistake." "He thought nothing could ever touch him." "You're not like that Stone."

"Sam was arrogant and made a huge mistake." "He thought nothing could ever touch him." "You can fix this, I know you." "You have a history of trustworthiness and you'll win them over one by one." Her smile was genuine and kind. "You just have to be real and convey to these people how sorry you are to them." "Then, she hesitated, move on." "This will be your office now." "You have this incredible opportunity to do some amazing things for Kentucky." "The men, women, and children of this state are depending on you for their future in jobs and education."

"Let's face it, Sam was a schmuck, but you're not." "Just believe in yourself and you'll be great!" Stone appreciated the go-team effort, but he couldn't let on what a wreck he was on the inside. His necktie felt like a tight noose around his neck, cutting off his breathing to shallow bits of air. He was sweating profusely through his shirt and underarms. His knees were trembling and he felt his heart inside his throat. It was just minutes before being thrown to the dogs, hungry overbearing reporters.

Stone fantasized what it could be like in four years if he pulled this off. Maybe I can do this, he thought. Stone was ready to offer a visionary and memorable speech to the people.

He flounced his boyish grin and grasped his hand tightly. "Let's do this!" he said with drummed up half-hearted confidence. Stone wasn't quite expecting what was coming next. Reporters were screaming at him from all sides. Nicole Jenkins knew how to make an entrance and that she did. A black limo pulled up and out stepped a beautiful blonde leggy woman. She was there to drop her bomb and stir up trouble as usual. There was nothing nice about Nicole. She saw her moment and lurched at it like a venomous snake hissing and ready to strike.

She flashed a wicked grin towards Stone and pushed him away from the microphone. "What are you doing Ms. Jenkins?" he said respectively. "You'll see, she whispered softly into his ear. "The people of the Commonwealth deserve to know the truth." The crowd became lethargic and somewhat dazed. They were hanging on her every word. "Governor Sam lied to the people of Kentucky and he killed my husband and Mattie McGraw's husband." "He did all this just to win an election."

Nicole was a great liar and came across so matter of fact. "He kidnapped Mattie's beautiful little girl, she's just a baby." "He tried to sell Melina and frame my sweet half-sister for murder." "Governor Sam was a dishonest man who stole the trust of the people and has ruined many lives."

"As I stand here today, one thing runs through my mind." "How can we possibly trust Stone Maupin?" "He was also the Governor's yes man to run this state honestly, effectively, and with integrity." "What I'm asking for is for the state election board to throw this election out and to start over." Stone was mortified. He never thought it would end like this. "What!" He flared a wicked glance towards her, but she was unmoved and unapologetic. He was furious with her for causing such an emotional scene.

"Lady you've got a lot of nerve!" What was she up to, he wondered. She continued. "My husband had a great vision for this state." She almost choked on her words. "I believe he would have been a great leader." "Miss Jenkins I'm truly sorry for your loss, but you can't do this." "Oh, I'm just getting started!" "I believe Kentuckians should get to decide again who would be a good leader for the state. "What are you saying Miss Jenkins?" "I am going to run for Governor and fill what should have been my husband's seat." "All I'm saying is let the people of Kentucky decide and vote again!" "We don't have a full investigation of the Governor and his new cabinet!" This made the new Governor to be very nervous. Nicole was sleeping and enjoying her bigger than life dream of taking over the Governor's mansion.

It didn't last long when she felt the plane shimmy and shake from side to side from an air pocket. It nearly took her breath away. She thought long and hard about her life and someday the consequences that would follow if her secrets were revealed. She thought about when she was a younger girl growing up in Beaver Dam. What life was like with her simple-minded parents, but they never appreciated her hopes and dreams. She always dreamed of being famous and successful. They were good people really, sincere and loving and kind. They raised her to have great compassion for other people and not to think of herself.

Her ambition was too strong and she vowed no one would stop from her getting what she wanted. She was daddy's little girl in every way. She worshipped him and wanted to connect with him, but he was hard to talk to. His commanding presence made her respect him and she rarely spoke back to him. He reminded her of King Kong. He was tall and strong and stood inverted. But his temper was not so nice. He didn't speak much, but if he had something to say, he spoke with clarity and relevance.

Her dad was also famous in Beaver Dam for getting thrown out of night clubs and being a bully when he was younger. He wasn't sorry for it, even the police were scared of him. Nicole loved the stories about his childhood.

Unfortunately, there was one secret about her father she would accidentally learn on her own. It would change her whole life. It creeped into her vision of what her life was supposed to be or what she thought it was. It changed her reality on everything. After her mother and father were killed in auto accident, she was on her own. The only one left in her family or so she thought. She was weeks away from being eighteen and ready to go off to Lexington on Seth Jenkins campaign. She was heartbroken for the loss, but getting out of Beaver Dam was the only way to keep her sanity and to erase her bad memories of what she had lost.

One day however, Nicole was rifling through her father's desk and found love letters, but not to her mother. Not just any woman, it was his mistress. It was a letter wrapped up in a red ribbon. She was floored. "My dearest Marilyn, you were the love of my life." "Watching her grow up would have been the thrill of my life, but I understand that is not possible." "I saw Mattie one day when I was dropping my own daughter off to school." "I was astounded at how much she favored my beautiful Nicole." "You have truly done a wonderful job of raising her." "She seemed so happy and grounded." "I also know that she has her problems here lately too." "I know I was supposed to stay out of her life, but I hired a private investigator to find out everything about her."

"I needed to know about Mattie." "She's a part of me after all." "A part of us." "We made this beautiful child." "I know about the pregnancy Marilyn." Nicole's jaw dropped and her heart sank with every word. "I have a sister, she repeated over and over. While most children might have been furious finding out their parent had an affair and a secret love child, Nicole was fascinated with the love affair. She was anticipating the day when she would finally meet the sister she had longed for. "My parents are dead, she sobbed.

"There's nothing my father can do to make this one right, she whispered. "He cheated on my poor clueless mother, who was always there for him, just like Betty Crocker." "His slave really, she cooked, she cleaned and kept his perfect little house just the way he liked it, spotless." "He was out cheating, living another life." Now her father seemed even more mysterious to her like a traveling gypsy who had no true roots. He never seemed very interested in his own family, his wife, or Nicole.

Nicole desperately wanted to be close to her father. She always had dreams of finding something that they would have in common and could share forever. Nicole's eyes nearly popped out of her head when she read the envelope and the address. She inhaled all of the excitement. "Mattie McGraw is my sister and she's having a baby!" "This would have been my father's first grandchild!"

She rifled through his office for hours until she came upon the investigator's report on Mattie. It included just about everything she wanted to know about Mattie McGraw. DOB 04-30-1966. Green eyes, brown hair. Weight 125 pounds. A light case of scoliosis. An A student, never in trouble with the police. She couldn't be my father's daughter, she thought. Her father was walking trouble with a brunt mouth and a big, hearty laugh. Nicole discovered Mattie was attending U.K. in the fall. Her father had obtained the doctor's files from Mattie's first obstetrician's visit up till the fourth month. He was really a sneaky rat.

Mattie was having a girl. The doctor's notes intrigued her the most. "Miss McGraw says the father is deceased and she is going to move to Lexington when the baby is born to raise the child." "Dr. McGowan also suggested giving up the baby for adoption, but she would not hear of it. Nicole felt sad for a moment. She never seemed to be her father's joy and it hurt her very deeply. As she continued to read through Mattie's files, she stumbled onto a very, very interesting picture of two lovers at the football stadium. Apparently, they were unaware of being photographed. They were wrapped around each other tightly gripping one another. The delight on their faces was effervescent.

It was Mattie McGraw and Jake Estevan. Nicole laughed gregariously over and over. "The playboy and Miss goody two shoes!" she laughed. "Mattie McGraw is having Jake Estevan's baby!" "Wait a minute!" "Jake's not dead!" It was like watching a slow movie unravel before her eyes. "Jake Estevan doesn't have a clue he's the baby's father!" "Aarggh!"

"Jake Estevan is definitely not dead!" "He doesn't know about the little blessing!" "And she doesn't want him to know!" "How deliciously sweet!" This was one little secret Nicole was keeping to herself. The next day she decided to pay the doctor a visit.

She simply made an appointment like everyone else. She was very, very nervous at first, but when he came through the door, she knew she had to have him in every way. He was forty-five with grayish-black charcoal hair with sparkling blue eyes. Their first visit went well. They were both automatically attracted to each other. They had nothing in common, except a baby.

Their relationship only lasted a few months. He felt guilty about cheating on his wife and ended it. Nicole didn't care, she had plenty of armor.

Lots and lots of pictures of them together, ready to use against him when the time was right. Dr. McGowan had no idea what kind of trouble he had gotten himself into. He was basically a good man. He felt very guilty about cheating on his wife. He begged Nicole not to tell her. Nicole agreed, but there would be a bigger price to pay for his adulterous affair at the end.

In the meantime, Nicole was busy preparing a home in Lexington for a small family. She planned everything very carefully. Since her parents died, she was left a very rich woman. The house, stocks, bonds and a life savings that would bring her many precious little things. She didn't care about staying in the house that suffocated all of her dreams and ambitions. The house sold very quickly on the market. In a few small months she would move into her elegantly decorated home.

Everything was falling into place for Nicole nicely. Her boyfriend after just a few short months, asked her to marry him. He was a very powerful man with big dreams as well and bent over backwards to please his new soon to be wife. Her new house was filled with many extravagant things, but Nicole was focused on one room. It was draped in pink and lavender, her favorite colors.

The room was filled with pink and lavender teddy bears and pink elephants and soon a beautiful baby girl that would be her daughter forever. Seth had no idea of Nicole's scheme to steal her half-sister's child. Seth was told there was a new mother who wanted to give the new baby up for adoption. He trusted Nicole with all the details, except he had to be there when the baby was born. Nicole insisted that the mother did not want to see them after the baby was born and that no meeting should take place. Even though Seth thought this was odd and wanted to thank her for the baby, he agreed to it.

When Mattie went into labor, the doctor was instructed to call her. When she gave birth, the baby would be quickly whisked away from her and would be placed into Nicole's awaiting arms outside the doctor's office. Nicole believed if Mattie never saw the baby, that this would be the most compassionate way to deal with the loss of her deceased child. Nicole always dreamed of being a mother and having a baby. She felt badly for Mattie, but her own selfish needs trumped everything else. After all, she thought, her sister had the one thing she could never quite get from her father, love and admiration.

CHAPTER 15

Revenge in the Bluegrass

A very solemn and sour Stone Maupin gave his speech to Kentuckians. There was sadness through all the Commonwealth. There was a heavy fog setting of doubtfulness and betrayal by the Governor. How appropriate Stone thought, on this really screwed up day. Stone felt so proud of the message he had hoped to convey to everyone. Better jobs, better education and a probing investigation into Sam's crimes and whereabouts. "I promise my fellow Kentuckians that for all the lies, mistrust, and scandals, Sam has brought you, I will replace it with truth and honesty." "All I'm asking you is a chance to prove myself worthy and to give me time to make things right that have been so wrong through all of this."

Madeline watched his graceful speech upstairs that he delivered with deep sincerity and true bravery. These people are out for someone's head on a platter, she thought. Then it was over in an instant and the sharks circled Stone like prey. Stone was covered in reporters from head to toe. The questions centered on Sam's quick exit and what he knew. "How could the people of Kentucky possibly have any trust in someone associated with Sam's administration?" The only thing missing were the imaginary stones being flung from every direction.

"What do you know about Sam leaving the country?" "Where is he?" "Did you have anything to do with Seth Jenkin's murder?" "Do you know who killed Ben McGraw?" "Where is Mattie McGraw and how does she fit into this?" The questions kept coming one by one, over and over. Stone was mortified and petrified and not sure which question to take on first. His assistant Ms. Cates stepped in. She was ready to hurl stones herself and kick ass. "We will answer one question at a time." She had presence for a very small lady and she was very annoyed by the reporters.

She pointed directly at one very surprised reporter. "Go ahead, she glared, we're not afraid to answer anything!" "And if we don't have an answer for you today, then we will surely get you one as soon as possible!" "Go ahead, she thwarted, ask your questions!" One of the reporters, first day on the job, blurted out like a rookie. "Where is Mattie McGraw and Melina and what does she have to do with this?" Before Stone could answer the question, Mattie and Melina appeared from the Governor's mansion to everyone's great surprise.

"I'm right here!" Mattie answered. She stood very calmly and poised ready to take on the piranhas that circled her and the new Governor. Mattie felt released from everything that had happened the past few weeks.

She wanted to help Stone and to make people realize Stone was the innocent one in all this confusion. She knew Ben's family would be watching and wanted them to know she was innocent too. She wanted the world to know her story from her mouth, not gossip, hearsay, late-night talk shows or anything else that spun out stories of make believe.

Jake grabbed Mattie to stop her. "You don't have to do this." He exclaimed. "You don't owe them anything!" "They were lied to by Sam, just like me." "They deserve to know my truth." Melina was resting peacefully in her mother's arms unaware the circus that was popping up around them. She carefully handed her to Jake. "Take her inside, I'll be right there." She reassured him. "Let me do this." She winked coyly at Jake and stepped up to the microphone. Stone was off to the side, relieved and happy he could breathe again. He hated confrontation and this was getting very ugly. He still wasn't sure if he could handle all of this, but for Mattie he damned well better try.

"A few weeks ago, she spoke softly. I thought I had been living the perfect life." "What I thought was perfect to me." Her eyes materialized on each face, she wanted each of them to truly get where she was coming from. "I was working for Governor Sam and discovered on my own accidentally some morose pictures of Seth Jenkins." "These were pictures obviously taken to prove he had been murdered." "When I confronted the Governor about it, he didn't deny it, he begged for my silence instead." "I knew I couldn't do it without a conscience." "I know now this was a very dangerous criminal." "So that's when I took the pictures and ran."

"I wasn't sure what I was going to do with them, so I ran home to the one person I knew would have answers." "I ran home to my husband Ben." "He was a lawyer and I knew he would know how to handle this situation." "He would have known who to give these damning photos to." "Unfortunately, it was too late when I got home." "I found my husband had been shot in the head and my daughter was taken from my home." She said with great sadness.

The reporters were mesmerized by her words and there was nothing but complete silence that encircled them. "You see, the Governor threatened me before I left." "He told me if I told anyone about Seth Jenkins or showed those horrific gruesome photos, I would be dead too."

"I was scared out of my mind!" "That's when I reached out to an old friend for help." Mattie looked at Jake with admiration and love. "He hid me for a few weeks until we were tracked down like dogs by officer Antonio Scollini." "He attempted to kill me and Jake, but we fought back and fled for our lives." "Jake and I have been on the run for weeks." "We've been trying to figure out why I had been set up for a crime I did not commit and where Melina was being held." "Luckily, I also had another friend."

"His name is Lil'J with the Kentucky State Troopers. They kept us safe and were helping me to clear my name." "He brought the FBI in and through their mutual investigation, they found my daughter Melina." Mattie was choking up as tears streamed down her face speaking of her baby. She took a deep breath and smiled brightly. "We were reunited today." The crowd applauded thunderously, which threw her. "I have my beautiful daughter back now, the most important thing in my life."

"Thanks to the FBI and to the Kentucky State Police all charges against me have been dropped." "But there is still a piece of this case that has not been solved yet." "Where is Governor Sam?" "When will he be found?" "I don't know that answer myself." "But what I can tell you is Stone Maupin, the FBI, and the KSP will find Sam."

"I have to believe that with all my heart." "All I'm saying to you is.... After all I've been through the past few weeks with this mess, is that you should give Stone a chance to fix this." "Give them a chance to get the answers we deserve from Sam." Lil'J wanted to protect his friend. He tapped her on the shoulder and she exited quietly. The reporters started barreling questions out again left and right till they were satisfied with all the answers.

Lil'J was going to make things right for Mattie again and he did. "Miss McGraw had absolutely nothing to do with any of this." "Mattie McGraw is an innocent woman who happened to be at the wrong place at the wrong time." He winked at her and finished the news conference. "This is all the information we have today and will release whatever findings that come to our attention." "Thank you."

A storm was coming. The clouds covered the sky. They were dark and gray moving slowly across the state. The wind was picking up again. Just as soon as Lil'J finished speaking, perfect timing he thought, the rain poured out of the sky like large pellets, sending reporters back to their news vans. Mattie and Jake and Melina flew into the Governor's mansion. They found a red velvet couch in the lobby and poured themselves into it.

"Mattie, I'm glad you got your daughter back." "Now everyone knows you're innocent, you deserved that." He grinned at her sheepishly. "See, I told you that the good guys always win." "Jake, you've been watching too many Westerns." "Aw shucks, ma'am." She smiled back half-heartedly. "That's great Jake, but what about all the bad guys in this?" "Do ya think they'll ever get theirs?" "Do they ever get caught?" "That's the thing Mattie...I can't figure it out." "Figure out what?" "Something's been bothering me the whole time about all of this." Mattie knew Jake had good instincts. She trusted him wholeheartedly.

"I can't help but think that there's more people involved in all of this." "Like who Jake?" "Oh, I don't know, Nicole Jenkins." "Her and Sam were awfully chummy at Seth Jenkins' funeral." "What if they both planned

his murder" "Why would she frame me?" "I don't know sweetheart."
"What if you were the wrong person, at the wrong place, the wrong time?"
"A lot of what if's I need to check out." "I need to go back to Beaver Dam,
where she's from." Mattie suddenly felt panic writhe through her veins.
"Why wouldn't the Governor be the first person to look for" "I mean if
you find Sam, wouldn't that give you the answers you need to solve this
case?" "No, Mattie I need to study Nicole Jenkins."

"I need to find out what makes her tick, her drives, her ambitions."
"You know it's weird she went to the same school we did, yet I don't
remember her at all." "I thought I knew everyone." "Do you know
much about Nicole Jenkins Mattie?" Mattie nervously looked up at the
ceiling away from Jake's eyes. One slip of the tongue and Jake would
know her deepest, darkest secrets. Mattie wanted to know the truth as
much as anyone.

The lies, the betrayal, Ben's murder and her baby being taken away
so cruelly from her. She craved justice for Ben and for all the torment
that Sam had put her through. But Mattie had her own secrets to protect
too. All she knew about Nicole was that she was her half-sister. They
never spoke, she never felt the urge to. Especially since she learned a
week before her graduation. The only reason her mother finally revealed
the truth, was that her real father had hired a private investigator to find
out about his daughter, he wanted to get to know her.

Apparently, it didn't matter he had made a pact with her mother to
stay out of Mattie's life forever. She begged Mattie for forgiveness for
cheating on her dad. She knew the affair was reckless and stupid and
promised her, never again. Mattie forgave her wholeheartedly.

Especially since she was pregnant with Jake's baby and planned
on never telling Jake. She was moving forward with a new life in
Lexington. Mattie felt horrible for keeping this from him, but she knew
he wasn't ready to be a dad and it wasn't fair to lay this on him. She
prayed someday he would understand and forgive her, just as she forgave
her mother for her tumultuous lies and betrayal.

CHAPTER 15

She was going places, getting ready to begin the University. She didn't want to hear about her mother and her lurid affair. She did however, want to protect her private information about the baby being born, she wasn't ready to spring that on Jake, not yet anyway. "I didn't really know her in high school, except I think I had a class with her." "I didn't really care for her smart mouth." "That I do remember." Mattie needed to work Jake real good, so this all wouldn't explode in her face. She felt so guilty for lying to Jake straight face. But she wanted to be there with him to detonate any bombs he was about to set off in Beaver Dam with their past on it.

Jake knew Mattie was lying. Her eyes were moving like a pinball machine, back and forth, up and down. She was a terrible liar. "What is she hiding?" "Why did she freak out when I mentioned digging up Nicole's history?" What's the connection he thought. Mattie had always been so neutral about Nicole. Jake pressed the gas pedal as far down as it would go. He carefully watched out for the Barney Fife's of Beaver Dam.

They loved to give Jake speeding tickets. Jake was perplexed by Mattie's behavior. He was completely enamored with her. He saw a real future with her down the road.

He never stopped loving her from the first moment her eyes met his. She meant everything to him. She was beautiful and sassy, just how he liked his Kentucky girl to be. She was daring and adventurous. Here lately though, very, very mysterious. Jake drove like a bat out of hell to get to his cabin. Luckily, Barney and Fife weren't paying attention to speeders today to see Jake brisk through Beaver Dam like a Nascar driver heading for the final lap.

He knew exactly what he was going to do. He pulled up to the cabin almost taking out his garage door. He ran into the house to the closet of shame and pulled out his electrician jumpsuit and his tool box. Jake loved playing the different characters his job required. Playing the bad girl in his gold sequin dress and stillettos still made him giggle. He was sneaky, but smart. No one knew it was even him. Boy, people are clueless, Jake thought. Jake grabbed a phone book and found Nicole's old address. Luckily, there was only one doctor in town that most of the women would go see. It was a very small town.

The women staggered over each other and would scratch each other's eyes out just for an appointment. Good ole' Dr. McGowan was every woman's fantasy in Beaver Dam. Jake hurriedly raced toward the door. He had places to go, people to see, secrets to uncover about Nicole Jenkins and Mattie McGraw.

This is the good stuff he thought. Excitement and lots of action. He grabbed for the door and it flew open. There she was, the most annoying…temperamental…high stressed woman he ever met. Mattie stood in the doorway with her arms crossed. "You didn't think I was going to let you do this without me did ya?" She stared at him contritely, which puzzled Jake. "I thought you were going to take Melina and spend some time with her." "She just got back, you know the mother daughter reunion." "Why aren't you with her?"

"She's fine, she's with my parents." "How do you know she'll be safe from the media or some crazy person that just wants to see Mattie the Madhatter and baby Melina?" "Jake, I've got it covered." "My mom and dad have security alarms in their house and the KSP is watching my house for a few days." "You know I wouldn't have left Melina if I didn't think it was absolutely necessary." "I trust my parents one-hundred percent." "Besides, if anyone tries to break in, my dad reassured me he would pull out his old buddy Remington steel." "How is Melina by the way?" She rolled her eyes.

"She's fine, my parents will spoil her rotten, I know she's safe and happy." "Nice outfit by the way." "Jake, I'm going with you." Jake raised his voice. "No, Mattie you're not!" He breezed past her fleeing to the car leaving her screaming at the top of her lungs and flailing her arms. Before he could get the key to the door, she toppled him to the ground like a sumo wrestler.

"Look, I have as much right to be here!" "I don't think Governor Sam did this alone either!" "I don't know why Nicole Jenkins would have anything to do with this, but I need some answers too!" She screamed. "Please, please let me help you Jake!" She looked at him authoritatively, pleading her case, not backing down. "Alright, alright, pushy woman, you can go, but stay quiet and stay out of my way!" Mattie grinned from ear to ear. Jake looked irritated with her, especially what happened in the cemetery. "I promise I won't be any trouble!" She said innocently enough. "Somehow I doubt that." "Alright fine, but if you're not on your best behavior, I'm leaving you out in the woods with the wild animals."

"I doubt that Jake, you and me we've become quite a team, she countered glowingly. "Besides the longer we wait, the longer it'll take to find Governor Sam and Nicole." Jake knew he was going to regret this, but a big part of him was happy to see Mattie. There was something so mysterious about her, yet forthcoming at the same time. He was anxious to uncover what secrets she owned as well. Mattie was like one gigantic jigsaw puzzle. Jake needed to piece together one piece at a time to truly understand her better. "Alright, he said almost defeated. He pointed towards the passenger side, get in before I change my mind." "But fair warning, if you cause any trouble, you're getting left out in the woods with the coyotes and bears." Mattie laughed hysterically.

They arrived at Dr. McGowan's office as the sun went down in Beaver Dam. Jake reached into his bag of tricks as he liked to refer to it. He pulled out very expensive pair of night binoculars to make sure everything was clear. Especially since they were breaking into the doctor's office. "Alright, he whispered, just stay low and stay behind me." "Got it!" he said sternly. "Yes boss, got it." They crept up slowly to the back door and Jake pulled out his anti-alarm device he ordered from the P.I. catalog. He was very proud of his toys. They made him feel like James Bond. It was a small metal device that he placed on the door that could disarm any alarm system.

When it came to getting into the door, that was the easiest, he pulled out his maxed out credit card and slid it between the door, the frame, and the door popped right open. Jake's heart was flying, he hadn't seen this much excitement in a very, long time. Nicole Jenkins enticed him almost as much as Mattie. "Alright, he pointed, get in fast."

Mattie obeyed and moved in quickly before Jake. For her, the doctor's office brought back lots of memories when she was pregnant with her and Jake's baby. "Stand right there!" "Hold onto the flashlight for me ok?" Mattie was non-responsive, standing in a daze-like stance flashing back to all those visits to Dr. McGowan's and preparing for her baby girl to be born. Jake was impatient and snapped at her.

"Mattie!" "What's wrong with you!" "You jumped me and begged to come with me!" "Are you with me or zoning out?" Mattie knew she had to pull it together fast. "I'm sorry Jake, you're right." "I was daydreaming for a minute, but I'm back now." She looked remorseful. "I'm sorry, women and their hormones, I'll never understand." "If you're not up to this, I'll take you back to the cabin!" "No, she pleaded. "I'm fine." "Let's do this!"

"I want to know what Nicole Jenkins has to do with all of this!" "Alright then, stay right there while I check Nicole's files." She nodded haphazardly. The office was decorated in pink flowers on the wall and the floors were draped with enormous mauve and white oriental rugs masking the shiny wooden floors. With every step they took, the floors creaked. Jake walked slowly into Dr. McGowan's office. It was dark except for the tiny ray of beams flowing through his flashlight. Normal, he thought. Everything looks like a doctor's office from his medical license from the University of Kentucky to the patient's table. In the corner was a file cabinet from A to Z. Jake grabbed Nicole's file and slammed it down on the desk.

Jake wondered if he was snooping on the right track. He hoped Dr. McGowan, since he was the most popular doctor in Beaver Dam, had secrets that would reveal themselves here. He gazed at a picture on the wall that didn't seem to fit.

The picture didn't match the décor of the room. It was a picture of Nice, France that displayed a French cafe. Also in the mix of the room there were hunting trophies and manly stuff. He questioned why would a manly man have a picture of Nice, France in his office, unless his wife bought it. A surge went up his spine. This was not a picture. Jake grinned from ear to ear, "So, what's the good doctor hiding?" Jake thought it was weird that very few people in Beaver Dam seemed to remember Nicole.

It seemed strange to Jake that Dr. McGowan gave one-hundred thousand dollars to Seth Jenkins campaign. Sure, a doctor has money, but one hundred thousand dollars was extravagant for even a small town country doctor. After carefully turning the combination left three times and two times to the right, the safe door popped open. A wide envelope lay flat on the safe floor. Maybe this was what he was looking for, Jake thought.

He carefully picked it up and dumped out the contents on the good Dr.'s desk. Mattie's heart raced. If only she could get to her file before all of her secrets spilled out before them. Bank receipts went flying and a check landed in Jake's hand. It was a check for ten-thousand dollars made out to Nicole Jenkins. Laying on the desk was even more scandalous.

It was a picture of Nicole and Dr. McGowan in bed together. Jake's mouth dropped. "Gotcha!" he declared. "It looks like the good doctor and Nicole were having an affair." "She was extorting money from him." "Hand me Nicole's file Mattie." She grabbed it first and breezed through it to the last few pages. Her eyes nearly popped out of her head as she almost dropped it. The last few paragraphs of the doctor's notes sent Mattie spinning. Paragraph 1: Nicole is in good condition, six months pregnant, baby's heartbeat is normal. Paragraph 2: Nicole is still in good condition, eight months pregnant. Baby's heartbeat is normal, weight gain 23 pounds. Paragraph 3: Gave birth to a healthy baby girl today. Everything was normal. Took baby home today.

Nurse Sweetin helped with the delivery and preparation of Mattie, Nicole Jenkins. The delivery date was 04-07-98.

CHAPTER 17

Even though she was under a lot of medications after she delivered her baby, Mattie remembered a baby crying and reached out to her. But Dr. McGowan reassured her that her baby died. Even in her drowsy condition, she could hear the baby crying. Then instantly, things went black again and she woke up a little later. The doctor and his nurse were hovering over her. "She looks good, he said patronly." "Real, good, good color." "Mattie you're going to be just fine." He smiled at her reassuringly and patted her head.

"Where's my baby Dr. McGowan?" "Where is she?" He hesitated for a moment, trying to think of the right way or the right words to break it to Mattie. "I'm so sorry Mattie, your little girl didn't make it." Mattie didn't know how to respond either. She was in shock. She wasn't exactly thrilled to be pregnant at eighteen years old. Although the last few weeks she had bonded with her baby, kicking her daily, keeping her up at night, sending her into a spiral of highs and lows. Emotions she had never dealt with before.

She felt it growing inside of her. She sat speechless, with blurred vision. Her body was tired, she felt like a train ran through her.

Dr. McGowan grabbed her hand and spoke ever so softly. He could sense the confusion in her eyes. She felt numb with despair and not quite sure how to handle this prolific news. Mattie was still hazy. "I heard my baby cry." She was insistent towards him. "No, no Mattie there was another mother who gave birth as well." "She was right next door." "She gave birth to a baby girl as well." "A baby girl!" Mattie demanded to know. "Oh, I'm sorry, but it was a baby girl."

"I heard my baby cry as soon as I gave birth to her!" "I know I'm not crazy!" The nurse stepped in to calm her down. Nurse Sweetin had a favorable demeanor. Her face was round and chunky, with caring blue eyes. Nurse Sweetin lowered her voice as well. "Matttie, sweetheart your baby was stillborn." "There was no heartbeat, no brain activity." "The crying you heard was next door when Harper was delivered." "Sometimes the medications can play tricks on you."

"Last month the test results showed that my baby was healthy, there was nothing wrong with her!" "Sometimes these things just happen." "No explanation whatsoever." "We're convinced that your baby had been stillborn for some time and in between visits it's hard to see something like this forthcoming." Mattie was heartbroken about the baby.

She was in no mood to argue with him. Maybe he was feeling guilty or just trying to be decent. She agreed. "What would you like to name her?" "Eva Catherine, she muttered. "Fine." Mattie decided she would say goodbye to Eva Catherine and this would be a forgotten memory. A memory to be put away like a precious treasure chest with lost loves. Mattie had a cold feeling about Nurse Sweetin. Anyone that smiles that much and speaks so sweetly must be tortured herself.

No one is that nice all the time, she thought. There was something callous about her underneath all that gobbledy-goop. She looked almost happy and relieved her baby died. What was she hiding, she wondered. Mattie promised herself to go on and find happiness in her young life, but Nurse Sweetin always haunted her.

She never took the opportunity to question her more, she just accepted Eva Catherine's death. She said goodbye to her a few days later at the Beaver Dam cemetery. She was appropriately dressed in a simple black dress, the tears flowed incessantly down her face. Mattie was grief stricken for her dead baby girl. She was coming around about being a young mother, but it was too late. She knew this was not meant to be. She placed a white plush teddy bear on her tombstone and said a prayer for her. "Mommy loves you forever." "Till we meet in heaven, sweet girl."

"Mattie, mattie" Jake snapped. "Where is your mind?" There was no good time to tell him about the baby, but now Mattie felt she had no choice. She didn't want to keep this secret anymore from the man she was falling in love with again. She decided to lay it all out for him. The pregnancy, their daughter's death. She looked up at him for reassurance, but Jake looked annoyed and so angry with her. She didn't care it was time to take a chance and let him decide if he could ever forgive her for keeping such a terrible secret. She grabbed his hand and looked solemnly into his eyes. "What is it Mattie?" "What's really bothering you?" "I have something to tell you." "I hope you can forgive me someday."

This would have to wait a little longer. Their silence was broken by the sounds of an opening door and a charging bull running down the hallway. Mattie and Jake stood frozen. Whatever escape they were forging, was too late. The earthquake stopped after a few seconds. The walls stopped shaking and a large, dark round figure appeared in the hallway flicking the lights on. It was an elderly woman in her fifty's. She was very stocky and sweating profusely. She looked furious and ready to blow up the place.

This would have been surprisingly funny to Jake if they hadn't got caught and the old lady wasn't dominating an aluminum baseball bat ready to swing at his head. There was nowhere to go and grandma was ready to attack. Jake carefully lifted his hands. "I can explain, he laughed. "It's a crazy story really." Jake gave her his best awshucks, cowby howdy doody grin, but she was not buying it. "I'm calling the police." "You two are going straight to jail." "That's funny Mrs. Sweetin, maybe you're the one that should be going to jail."

"Madeline?" "Is that you dear?" "Yes, Mattie McGraw." "Please put the bat down Mrs. Sweetin." "We mean you no harm." Mrs. Sweetin reluctantly dropped the black and silver aluminum bat onto the floor. "Let me handle this one Jake." "Mrs. Sweetin you remember me, don't you?" The truth about the baby was going to come out, now was good as time as any. She knew Jake may never speak to her again, but she was willing to take that chance.

No more lies, he deserves to know about his baby girl. Mrs. Sweetin put her hand on Mattie's face stroking it gently. "Poor girl, I'm glad to hear you were able to have children." She said sincerely to Mattie as if she were her own child. Mrs. Sweetin was holding a terrible secret of her own for seven years now. It haunted her day and night. She remembered the day Mattie gave birth to her beautiful little girl.

She was healthy and she was crying for her mother. Nurse Sweetin prayed that God would forgive her for giving Mattie's baby to Nicole Jenkins. The baby cried for her mother loudly. She was spineless, she followed the doctor's instructions to the note. Clean the baby, walk to the back door and hand her to her new mother, Nicole Jenkins. Nurse Sweetin wanted so badly to stop this incredible injustice against Mattie. She disliked Nicole Jenkins profusely. There was nothing to like about her, she knew Nicole set this in motion. She knew about the affair with Dr. McGowan and oh yes, the blackmail. There wasn't anything in the office she didn't know about. She truly believed Dr. McGowan was a good man forced into making a terrible, terrible mistake.

She needed her job, so selfishly she went along with the plan. She kept this terrible secret to herself and to protect Dr. McGowan. She hoped someday to tell Mattie about her baby if Dr. McGowan passed away before she did. When Nurse Sweetin heard about Mattie's baby Melina she almost gave in. However, she decided not to tell her when she got Melina back. She reckoned bad things in the past were better left behind. For seven years she feared this day would come and she would have to accept her part in this. Emotions were running high between them. "Another baby, what is she talking about Mattie?" Jake queried.

Nurse Sweetin was pale with fear. She looked at Mattie with sorrowful eyes and deep regret. "I'm so sorry Mattie." "I'm so, so, so, sorry for your loss." "That happened a long time ago, I have moved on." "Maybe it was for the best." "I was very young and not quite ready to be a mother yet." Mattie couldn't understand why Nurse Sweetin was bringing this up. She seemed to be taking this very hard. Jake was flabbergasted. He thought he knew everything about her. "You were pregnant seven years ago." "You had a baby and lost it?" That was a lot to take in. "Hold on a minute Jake."

"I guess Mrs. Sweetin you want to know why we're here." She was redirecting this train wreck fast, but Jake interrupted. "You can't blow this off Mattie!" "I'm...I'm not!" "Let's just all calm down first!" "Fine, he snapped. "But I'm not letting this one go understand?" "I'll tell you everything!" Mattie responded. "First things first!" "Mrs. Sweetin, we believe Nicole Jenkins had something to do with her husband's murder, the blackmail, and setting me up." "Mrs. Sweetin, what do you know about Nicole Jenkins?" Jake was infuriated with both of them. "I would answer very carefully if I were you." He picked up the picture of Dr. McGowan and Nicole. Nurse Sweetin grabbed a swivel chair and slowly placed herself into it.

She exhaled slowly as if it were her last breath. "I'll tell you everything I know." "It was going to come out some day anyway." "I just wanted to protect Mattie from all the pain." "I know she's been through so much already." "Mrs. Sweetin what did Nicole Jenkins have on Dr. McGowan?" "Besides their affair?" "I never wanted to hurt you Mattie." "I didn't want to do it." "Dr. McGowan was afraid of losing everything." "I know he was afraid of his wife finding out about the affair." "Losing his reputation, his business, his life as he knew it."

"Mrs. Sweetin you're not making any sense." "Get to the point!" "When that girl stepped into his life, she almost destroyed everything." "She knew what she wanted from the start." "She had it already planned." "What did she have planned Nurse Sweetin?" "What did she want?" She shook her head from side to side. "No......no......no..... I can't" She was grief stricken and so sorry for all the pain she was about to unload on Mattie. Jake was adamant toward Mrs. Sweetin. "Look at me!" "You're not getting out of this room or that chair till you tell us everything!" Mrs. Sweetin cowered in fear. "Now again, what was Nicole looking for?" "Why did she blackmail Dr. McGowan and how did you get dragged into all of this?"

She gazed at Mattie for some sort of sign, what to say, that she could be forgiven, but Mattie stood motionless glaring at her. Mrs. Sweetin folded her arms over her chest like an armor that could protect her, but she knew the truth needed to come out, whether she was ready or not. He was growing impatient with her and leaned into her slowly. "What was Nicole Jenkins looking for!" "Uh, uh a baby." "Whose baby, Jake snarled at her. Ms. Sweetin tightened the grip around her chest, looking to Mattie for help. Mattie pushed Jake back and stepped in toward her and grabbed her hand. This good cop, bad cop wasn't working for her.

She decided the situation needed a softer touch and Jake was scaring the poor woman to death, she thought. "Please Mrs. Sweetin, we think Nicole Jenkins set me up for Seth Jenkin's murder and my husband Ben. "If you know something, you have to tell us." "It's ok whatever it is, we'll protect you from her." That's just what Mrs. Sweetin needed to hear, a kind word from Mattie, even though she knew she didn't deserve her sympathy. "Whose baby was Nicole looking for?"

"Nicole wanted your baby Mattie." "She found out you were her half-sister and you were pregnant. "Mattie had been through so much with Ben's murder, being attacked by Scollini, she wondered if she would survive. Also, losing Melina and not knowing if she would ever find her.

When she visited Ben's grave at the cemetery, she felt some sort of peace. Then Melina came back to her. She felt stronger and just maybe she thought, things were going to be alright. But the words from Mrs. Sweetin burned her face and sent her into a fiery rage. Mattie completely lost herself and gave into her animal rage. She dove for the nurse and they both fell onto the floor. Her strong hands were wound tightly around Nurse Sweetin's neck. Mattie was like a great white shark attacking their prey during lunch time. Unforgiving and reckless. Nurse Sweetin's head bobbed back and forth wildly, almost taking her breath away.

"Mattie she's not worth it." He tried reasoning with her, but she wasn't listening. Finally, a cold, hard smack across Mattie's face did the trick. He pulled her off Nurse Sweetin. She was disheveled and breathless. He grabbed Mattie's shoulders and shook her violently. "Listen to me!" "I know this is bad, but we need to hear this!" "She told me my baby died!" He tightly wrapped his arms around her to calm her down. Jake gently stroked her hair and kissed her wet, moist face. "Go on, Mrs. Sweetin, she nodded. "Mattie was heavily sedated going in and out of consciousness." "The baby girl that was born that night was healthy, there was nothing wrong with her."

"I cleaned her up and walked to the back door, she said sheepishly. "I handed her to Nicole and her boyfriend Seth Jenkins and they drove away." "I never saw her again after that." "Dr. McGowan said it would be best not to ever bring this up again and to keep quiet." "So, I did what he asked me to do." "I know it was wrong." "I'm so, so sorry I gave your baby away, she said with remorse. Tears drizzled down her face as she spoke, but a heavy burden had been lifted from her shoulders. It felt good to finally let it go.

She was ready to deal with the consequences now. A s the police car drove away, Mattie and Jake stood together in silence for a moment. Just when she thought all bad things were coming to an end, this was just the beginning of another intrepid storm that was about to blow her life to pieces. "You were pregnant that summer we spent together, he said solemnly. "Yeah, she answered haphazardly. He asked her the question he already knew the answer to. "Was that baby girl mine?" She looked at him apologetically. "Yes Jake, that baby girl was ours." "I didn't think you were ready to be a dad and I wasn't ready to be a mom." "I was planning on keeping her and raising her anyway." "Can you ever forgive me for not telling you?"

"You mean lying to me and keeping the baby a secret?" Jake was hurt, but not really mad at her. He could never stay mad at her. "You're right, I wasn't ready to be a dad back then." "But somewhere out there Mattie, we have a little girl that's being raised by a psychopath." "I know Jake." "What are we going to do about that?" "I'll tell you what we're going to do." "We're going to search the world and bring our daughter back." They looked at each other wistfully, each carrying the pain of losing a child. Jake and Mattie sobbed together quietly holding each other tightly and mourning the past seven years. What might have been or could have been a great life with their daughter. They were united on the search for her and vowed to never stop looking for their little girl.

CHAPTER 18

$\mathcal{M}$ eanwhile in Nice, France............
On the Mediterranean in Nice, France is a beautiful country surrounded by Monte Carlo, where the rich play. They sunbathe on the sandy pebble beaches in the nude, dining on Meditteranean pasta and gambling in the casinos all night. Governor Sam had almost wiped out his intrepid past in Kentucky. He had taken on a new identity that was unrecognizable. His hair was smoky gray colored with jet black lines and a mustache. Lenny constantly reminded him to watch his back and not to get to close to anyone.

This was hard for Sam because he was fun-loving, warm, funny, and loved to tell stories about his so-called past. Sam was very careful to rearrange important facts in his stories. Especially those concerning his position of power and why he ended up in Nice. The story he spun was of an early retirement and he decided to buy a vineyard. This concerned Lenny however, who worried for them both and their protection.

The private investigator had been reporting back to Nicole Jenkins for weeks. He watched every move the Governor and Lenny made. They were late risers. At ten every morning they drank cappuccinos and ate croissants at La Bleu Café by the ocean.

They read the paper for international and local news while discussing politics, the weather, and Lenny's plan to purchase a winery in the country. By eleven, they both sunbathed on the endless pebble beach till three. At five they walked the streets soaking up the history of Nice. They visited museums and the finer restaurants drinking cabernet and eating escargos and lagostinos. By eight, they were appropriately dressed in tailored black and white suits heading for the casinos in Monte Carlo.

They spent hours gambling and heading back to the villa by one am. Lenny was insistent on moving him and the Governor into the country where they would be more protected and out of sight. Sam liked things the way they were and didn't worry because that was Lenny's job. Lenny reminded Sam daily, one wrong mistake, one word could bring them both down. Sam just wouldn't listen and ignored his pleas to be more careful. He was untouchable, he thought.

After one exciting night of casino gambling, heavy drinking and meeting with the ladies, Sam and Lenny were ready to call it a night and head back to their villa. They never separated from each other for very long. Lenny insisted on it. Sam understood the validity of Lenny's concerns. He hoped someday he could break free of Lenny and live freely alone.

Sam always had a plan and a huge bank account in Switzerland and in Italy. Sam loved Lenny as a brother. He realized the great sacrifice he made for him. Sam would die for Lenny if he had to. Lenny was loyal and held the many dark secrets Sam kept from everyone. He was his trusted confidante who risked his life and gave up his own life of normalcy.

As they strolled through the door, Sam hoped with some gentle nudging, he could convince Lenny to go back to his own life and release him of any responsibility for him. "You know old friend, you've given up a lot so I could be free." "But I want you to go back to a normal life." Another voice echoed from the sun porch. A shadowy figure stepped out of the dark. "I couldn't agree more Sam." "Nicole what are you doing here?" "How did you find us?" "Well it wasn't that hard." Nicole rolled her eyes. "I hired a private investigator." "He's been watching you two for weeks."

Lenny was slowly becoming unraveled. He despised Nicole Jenkins almost as much as he despised her husband Seth. "You're the one that got Sam into this whole mess." "Oh, believe me she said playfully, Sam was a willing partner." "I doubt that!" Lenny snarled. "What do you want Nicole?" Sam fired at her expeditiously. "Well the plans have changed Sam." "I can't have you walking around messing things up for me."

"Sam, you never know when to keep your mouth shut." "It's too risky." "I can't have you bringing me down with you." "After all, I have a daughter to raise." "You mean Mattie's daughter." "You cold-hearted witch!" "Weren't you the one who tried to sell her daughter to that witless couple in Switzerland?" "I was just covering my tracks." "I was trying to give Melina a good life." "Touche!" "That's your problem Sam, you need a cleaner to scour your messes." "I know how to make mine go away."

You're in this as much as me!" "You came to me to take care of your husband!" "Mattie should never have been involved!" "She was like a daughter to me!" "How touching!" "I'll tell anyone who will listen to me that this was all you!" "Oh, Sam who would believe you?" "Everyone knows you're a crook, a thief, and a big fat liar." "Besides I am the grieving widow who dearly loved her husband." "That's a stretch!" snapped Lenny. "Wait a minute, Sam we've got to get out of here."

"She's already called the police." "All of this crazy bantering back and forth." "Nicole was counting on it." She smiled wickedly across the room. "You won't make it gentlemen." Lenny and Sam looked at each other with panic stricken eyes. Consequently, Lenny was always the cool headed one. He knew how to strategize a hot mess. That was his forte. Sam, on the other hand, knew how to panic really well and cry like a baby.

Sam could never handle stress very well. "Sam, you're my best friend, but I'm so tired of pulling your but out of the fire." "Sorry Sam, but I'm not going to spend the rest of my life in jail with you." Nicole was intrigued. "Lenny, you'll never make it." "The police will be here any minute." Lenny grabbed the remote control and pushed lots of buttons and the living room wall opened. Inside their villa Lenny had installed a secret getaway room like Batman.

He opened the closet and grabbed a painter's suit with blue overalls and a painter's cap and boots. He quickly changed. Sam was speechless, but he knew Lenny was right. He deserved to be free and to be no part of what Sam had done. This was all his mistakes and it was time to pay for them. "Sam, I'll send you legal help, but remember it's not over till the fat lady sings." "Don't despair, you'll be alright." "Get out of here as fast as you can and don't look back!" "I'll be fine, take care of yourself."

Lenny felt real bad for leaving Sam high and dry, but he had to flee this crazy mess. He gave Sam a big bear hug and took off for the secret getaway and quickly the wall closed behind him. He was gone. Sam was saddened by the loss of his friend. He really thought things were going to be ok. He was living the life he always dreamed of, but the past has a way of catching up on you.

"What's going through your mind Sam?" Nicole asked. "Are you thinking of fleeing too?" "Don't worry Nicole, you'll get yours someday." "I'm truly sorry for all the bad things I've done and I pray to God for forgiveness of all my sins." "Oh Sam, I think there's a spot waiting for you in hell." "You first Nicole." "Don't you care for all the horrible things you've done?" Nicole rolled her eyes at Sam. "You wanted Seth dead as much as I did!" "Remember?" "You were in a panic that he was going to take your place as Governor and erase everything you had accomplished."

"He was a horrible, horrible man who didn't care about anyone else but himself." "Scollini did us all a favor." Sam knew it was no use talking to her, she had no soul. He was staring at a cold-hearted, scornful, bitter woman. "What about Mattie?" "She's your sister." "Half-sister, she retorted. "Sometimes I feel sorry for her, but she had the life I always wanted." "I thought my father loved her more than me." She said sarcastically. "She was a winner." "Everything she touched turned to gold."

"When I was a little girl, I could never understand why my father showed no interest in our family." "Then I found out about his affair with that other woman." "He wanted them more." "He loved them more."

"I just took what should have been mine to begin with." "Mattie's a very smart girl, she'll figure it all out someday with my help." "I don't think so Sam." "You won't be here to tell your side of the story." "You'll be dead!" "Sam, you didn't think I was going to let you take me down with you did you?" Nicole slowly pulled out a .38 pistol pointing it directly at Sam's chest. "What about the police, they'll be here any minute." "It was self-defense, you came at me and I was terrified for my life!" She began destroying the living room and knocking over chairs. The glass tables shattered into thousands of pieces.

"There was a terrible fight." She ripped her dress off her shoulder and punched her eye with her fist several times. "We struggled, luckily you dropped your gun and I grabbed it away from you." "I knew if I didn't shoot you I would be dead." She tightened her grip on the gun. Sam looked terrified and was ready for all of this to be over. "Any last words Governor?" "Wait, wait we can work this out, I'll keep my mouth shut, I promise."

"I want to live Nicole, I know I don't deserve to live for all the people I hurt." "What do you say Nicole?" "Let me go and you'll never hear from me again." "I promise you that!" Sam pleaded with her for mercy. "Good night Sam!" she responded. She fired two bullets into Sam's chest and he hit the floor hard. "Lights out Governor."

The French police showed up just a few moments later, horns blaring, surrounding the villa. Lt. Thacker and his men surrounded each corner of the villa ready to shoot at any moment. They anticipated the worst. Lt. Thacker shouted from the bull horn, Governor it's all over." "Put your hands up and walk out of the door slowly." He repeated this several times, but there was silence. He kicked the door open, not knowing what to expect, but ready for a tumultuous showdown.

Instead, there stood Nicole with her hands up in the air crying and shaking violently. Sam was spread out on the floor bleeding and unresponsive. The Lt. checked to see if Sam was still alive. "There's a pulse." "Get an ambulance here fast!" He shouted to his men. "I found him and told him it was all over!" Nicole blurted out. "I told him I called you and you were on your way." "That's when he tried to attack me and kill me!" "I had no choice!" Nicole knew how to play the sympathy role well. Lt. Thacker reached out his hand slowly to Nicole.

"Just calm down Nicole and give me the gun." "You believe me, don't you?" "It's all over now, he said calmly. "He can't hurt you anymore." She stretched out her hand slowly shaking from side to side and Lt. Thacker grabbed the gun and put it carefully into a plastic bag for evidence.

"Did I not tell you to stay from here?" "Yes, but I was outside watching the villa." "I couldn't let them get away." "I told them you were on your way." "Lenny escaped through that wall." "It's a secret getaway." Lt. Thacker looked at Nicole with disbelief and the realization that this was a very unstable woman or a very calculating one. "I'm sure it does." He said reassuredly. "Take the remote, it opens the wall." He grabbed the remote to humor her. He started pushing buttons, the lights flickered on and off. Lt. Thacker was amazed when the doors opened and closed and the wall opened up completely.

Lt. Thacker and his men were astounded. "They were prepared for this day it would seem." The crazy lady was telling the truth, he thought. "Nicole we'll work this out at the police station." "You have a lot of explaining to do." Nicole sat sheepishly at the police station offering her version of her story. Lt. Thacker wasn't so sure. In another room, he and his sergeant discussed what to do with Nicole. "I think she's lying through her teeth!" "I think she came to Nice for revenge for the death of her husband."

"Lt. Thacker had a gut feeling about her and her story. Sergeant Drupe wasn't so sure. "You may be right, but we can't prove it." "Why would she call the police if she had every intention to kill Sam and let us find him dead?" "Yes, her story seems unbelievable, but she also has another reason to be here."

"She has a little girl in a boarding school here." She says she was coming to pick her up." "Why would she risk jail and not be able to take her daughter home?" "Lt. Thacker we already have a huge circus on our hands." "What are you suggesting Sargeant Drupe?" "The man who started this has been shot and may die." "I say we escort Ms. Jenkins out of the country with her daughter." "What!" Lt. Thacker screamed in disbelief. "We don't have enough proof to hold her!" "We'll cross our fingers and visit Sam."

"Hopefully he can clear this up." "If he lives." "We'll keep her under surveillance until we speak to Sam." "Just escort her back to her hotel." "We'll take her to the airport and make sure she leaves the country with her daughter, if Sam tells the same story." "Ms. Jenkins, you may go, after you pick up your daughter tomorrow." "This has created quite a media circus." "We will escort you both to the airport."

"That won't be necessary." Nicole exclaimed. "Oh, but I insist Ms. Jenkins." "We will also be escorting you back to your hotel." "I heavily recommend that you stay out of the public eye until you leave." "If that's what you think is best." She gave him a half-hearted smile. Nicole was a world-wide phenomenon. The story broke about the vengeful widow taking justice into her own hands.

From Italy to Rome and back into the U.S. When she walked out of the police station, she was surrounded by reporters shoving microphones in her face and cameras flashing from all sides. Her large round black Adrienne Vittadini glasses covered her black eyes. They could not hide the exuberant feeling she had. Getting away with the perfect crime was euphoric. She felt a surge power resonate through her body.

Tomorrow she would pick up Nicolette and go home to her Italian lover. She was going to have it all. Life would be perfect she thought. "No one can stop me now, she whispered to herself." Unfortunately, there was one obstacle in her way. Still alive and breathing and ready to take her down with him. Governor Sam was still alive according to news reports from her phone. Nicole began devising the perfect plan to pay Sam a little visit under the police radar. "This time Sam, you won't be so lucky." Things were going well for her, she loved her life. "Why should Sam screw it all up for me?" This time she would finish the job she started.

CHAPTER 19

As Mattie and Jake flew over the Atlantic Ocean, she received several text messages from Lil'J. She and Jake were unaware of the shooting in Nice. Text: Mattie, Governor Sam was found shot in Nice, France. Apparently, Nicole Jenkins tracked him down and was the shooter. She was taken into police custody and released on her own recognizance. The police and Interpol have put her under a twenty-four hour surveillance.

She's also being escorted out of the country with her daughter tomorrow. I know what you're thinking already. Stay out of it and let them deal with this. Congratulations on getting Melina back. I know you're excited. I will keep you informed and updated. Take care, stay close and don't be a stranger.

Sincerely, Lil'J "She's leaving the country with our daughter, our daughter!" "Over my dead body!" Jake snapped. Jake read the text from Lil'J trying not to show much emotion. Mattie was upset enough for the both. He gripped her hand. "Nicole's leaving the country with our daughter Jake!" She gasped for air. He looked at her with his serene brown eyes gazing into hers. "No baby, we won't let her get away with this!" "We have all the evidence we need."

"The pictures, the check, the confession from Nurse Sweetin." "What if we don't get there in time?" "What if she gets away with our little girl?" "Don't cry Mattie!" "I promise you...........tears rolled down her face. "Look at me!" He grabbed her face to gently reassure her. "I promise you we will find Nicole and we will find our little girl and bring her back with us." Mattie was obviously shaken from the news. "Jake, I can't lose another daughter, I just can't take it!" "Nicole is already there, she knows the city, she knows how to get around." "She's already ten steps ahead of us."

"That's true, but she probably didn't count on the Governor being alive." "As soon as we land, we'll pay Sam a visit and find out if he knows where our girl is." "Remember we're the good guys and the good guys always win." Mattie lay her head on his shoulder for reassurance and to prepare for a trip she would never forget. While Mattie lay sleeping on Jake's shoulder, Jake made some preparations of his own. He scalped Mattie's phone and made a call back to Lil'J.

"Jake you and Mattie have no business in Nice." "Let the police handle it!" "Can't do that Lil'J." "There's an important part to this puzzle that you're all missing." Jake told Lil'J about the blackmail envelope found in Dr. McGowan's office and the nurse's confession about giving Mattie's baby to Nicole Jenkins. "Apparently Mattie and Nicole are half-sisters."

know Mattie had another girl." "We just found out we are both parents." "She was our little girl, Lil'J." "They told Mattie the baby died." "The police in Kentucky agreed to keep this quiet until they can find Dr. McGowan and Nicole and our daughter." "I need a favor from you." "Yeah, yeah sure, anything for you guys." "I need you to contact the police in Nice, since you have contacts." "Have them meet us there at the airport."

"Nicole found out Mattie was pregnant and wanted her baby." "Oh gosh, I didn't know Mattie had another girl." Jake reflected back.

"We need to talk to Sam and find out where our daughter is." "Done." "I can't let Nicole take our daughter out of the country." "We're dealing with a killer here, Lil'J." "If she gets away, she'll kill again." "I'm sure of it." As Mattie and Jake were entering Nice they were unaware of the celebration taking place. Crowds of people were gathering in the streets. They were dancing and drinking chardonnay. They were eagerly awaiting the intrusion of race car drivers from all around the world for the Grand Prix.

Jake reflected to the past few months with Mattie. Before she fell back into his life, he was a one man show. A life filled with meaningless jobs and meaningless one-night stands. He always felt like something was missing from his life. Now he couldn't imagine another day without Madeline McGraw. She made him feel whole again.

She completed him in so many ways. She challenged him. She was the love of his life. He wanted to spend the rest of his life with her in his arms. Now he was going to be a father to a little girl he never knew existed. He hoped Mattie would show him how to be a good dad. He prayed to God for guidance and direction and for the good guys to win.

At the hotel Nicole sat patiently planning her next move. Going back to Kentucky was not an option anymore. She loved the Bluegrass, it was her home. She adored the galas, the derby parties and mixing and mingling with the Southern gentlemen. However, she was ready for a new start somewhere entirely new with her daughter Nicolette. Now that Sam was taken care of, she could start fresh where no one could recognize her and Nicolette.

Spain was her first choice. She loved the culture, the cuisine and the beautiful landscapes. Greece always intrigued her as well. She dreamed of doing the happy dance and smashing plates everywhere. It was an old Greek tradition. She was more interested in the men. Especially the dark tanned Meditteranean greek gods, she smiled. Nicole was rich, beautiful and smart. She was used to getting what she wanted and more.

She was never satisfied with what she had. She always wanted more. Her appetite for men was insatiable.

"Oh, my darling Nicolette, mommy loves you, but soon you are going back to school." "Mommy's free and wants to play with the boys." Nicole wasn't cut out to be a mother. She liked the idea of it all, but she was too selfish and self-centered to be a good mother. Seth knew this when he married her, but he let her have her little dream and she knew it. She barely paid any attention to the little girl, unless there was a photo opportunity or to show her off to her rich, impressionable politicos.

Nicolette loved her father even though he could be harsh at times, but she loved her nannies even more. They were more like a mother to her than her very own. After five years of having a child in the house, Nicole decided it was time for Nicolette to go. She made the arrangements, much to her daughter's chagrin. She waited for the right time when Seth was on one of his political venues. She knew Seth would never go for it.

She took Nicolette to a boarding school in Nice, France. She knew it would really sting Seth especially since they spent their honeymoon there. Nicolette cried and pleaded with her mother the whole trip. "Mommy, mommy please don't take me away from Daddy!" Nicole ignored her pleas.

"You'll love France sweetheart, you'll learn new things and make new friends." "I'm doing this for you, so you'll be well educated." Nicole just wanted her gone secretly. When Seth returned from his speaking engagements in Frankfort, the house was quiet. It seemed empty. No thunderous laughs roaring through the house. All he wanted to do was scoop Nicolette up in his arms and make funny faces with her. "Daddy's home Nicolette come and see me." "Come to Daddy!" There was no response, dead silence. "Nicole, Nicolette where's my girls?" He began to worry a little bit, but then he remembered Nicole was home with their daughter.

He figured they were spending time together since the maids and nanny were nowhere in sight. He was so excited to share with Nicole the good news. He was climbing in the polls and getting closer and closer to defeating Sam. Everything looked great. It didn't hurt either knowing that Sam paid for votes and he was going to bring that up in the next debate. He was still going on adrenaline from his stump speeches and the support of his followers.

As he set down to fumble through the paper, the smell of steak filled the air. "Nicole, where are you?" Steak was his favorite meal. He smiled grandly. "I'm right here sweetheart." "Could this day be any better?"

Especially since it's your last night, she thought. Nicole stepped out of the kitchen and posed in front of Seth like a supermodel facing the flashing cameras with a sweet smile. "Hello sweetheart." She brought him his favorite glass of peach iced tea and kissed him gently on the forehead. Seth never drank, he was against it completely. Nicole had her fill of wine before he got home. That's the only way she knew she could pull this off. She dreaded him coming home.

Kissing him made her almost physically sick. The thought of her husband touching her made her want to throw up. He was like a vile snake to her. The only time he was nice or played nice was when things were going well for him. Besides, he paid more attention to Nicolette than me, she thought. "I made your favorite dinner since it will be your last." She murmured. She thought about poisoning him and watching his head hit the table at dinner. But she couldn't in any way be linked to his death. Tonight, she would play the happy wife and mother. After all, he'll be dead tomorrow. She thought. She knew Seth would be very angry about Nicolette, but there was nothing he could do about it. For once in her life, the cards were stacked in her favor and she reveled in it. She grabbed his arms and led him to the dining room for dinner.

"Come and git it!" She said with a twang. "Tell me about your day honey." Something weird was going on here. This was not like Nicole. She always let the maids cook dinner and the nanny took care of Nicolette. "I didn't know you could cook anything." "Oh darling, I could do lots of things you could never have imagined." She grinned ever so slightly. She was dressed in her most sexiest black dress, sleeveless with crisscross straps in the back, very, very short.

She wanted his whole attention on her and it worked for a little while. "Where's Nicolette, Nicole?" "Secondly, what do you want?" "You never cook for me and you only wear that dress when you want to impress." "Nicolette is fine, she wasn't ready to drop the news on him just yet about her departure. "Maybe I just wanted a quiet dinner with my husband." "Fine, where's our daughter?" "Off with the nanny?" "Mmmmm......hmmmmm....I wore this dress for you do you like it?"

He plunged his fork and knife into his steak eating little bits, so he could savor each bite. Seth had a great day and he wasn't about to let Nicole ruin it. He was tired of her insecurities and manipulative behavior. He usually gave in to whatever she wanted, but it never seemed to be enough for her. She wanted the big house like Dallas, he bought it for her.

He spent almost his last dime to buy it. Then she wanted the mink coat, even though he thought it was overly tacky and showy, he bought it. He needed peace tonight, so he gave her what she wanted. "Of, course Nicole, you always look sexy in that black dress or anything you wear." "But how many times have I told you how beautiful you are?" "She looked annoyed, stabbing him with a fork didn't sound like a bad idea after all.

Then she took a deep breath and exhaled slowly. "I just don't understand why I have to drag it out of you every time." "I would think it would come naturally for you to compliment your wife." "Nicole I've told you hundreds of times how beautiful you are." "Yes, ok, well enough of that subject, alright." She agreed. "How was your day?" "Great!"

He smiled. "I'm climbing in the polls."

"Looks like in November we'll have a new home honey!" You'll have a new home tomorrow, five feet under she smiled. Nicole just kept reminding herself of tomorrow. She felt happy and jubilant. Seth would be dead and she would be free of him forever. She knew the subject of Nicolette was coming, so she braced herself for the storm to come. "Where's our daughter?" He demanded. "When will she be back with the nanny?"

"I've decided Nicolette needed a better education and we need more time together." She just blurted it out. "She's in a boarding school in Nice, France she said matter of fact. "What!" Seth pounded the table, but he wanted to pound Nicole. "We never discussed this!" "Why would you take our daughter all the way across the ocean away from her parents?" "She's only seven years old!"

He bellowed at the top of his lungs and the words echoed throughout the house. "Oh, dear God!" "Nicolette must be petrified being taken out of her home!" He was livid with her. He leaned all the way across the table and Nicole jumped.

Seth adored Nicolette, she was the only thing that kept him from divorcing Nicole. He looked wistfully out the window. "I thought if I gave you a child, you would want to be a mother and a good wife, and we could be a happy family!" "Apparently self-centered, selfish Nicole got tired of having a child in the house, a child she ignores most of the time." "A child who is closer to me and her nanny." He swung around and faced her contemptuously.

This was it, Nicole had done the unthinkable, he would divorce her after the election. Nicole sat calmly, not moving, not even a flinch.

She was barely breathing. "Seth, please try to understand." "Shut up!" "I've given you everything you've always wanted!" "This little girl did nothing to you!" "All she ever wanted was to be loved by her mommy and daddy!" "You just couldn't do that could you?"

His face was red with anger and resentment towards her. "You never wanted a baby!" "That's not true!" "I held her every chance I could." "Please don't do this to me Seth!" Nicole turned away, but he got in her space. He tried to speak with her in terms she would understand. "I sang to her when she was an infant Nicole!" "You remember that!" He was trying to trip some kind of emotion from her, to make her realize the colossal mistake she just made.

Tears streamed down her face and she held her head down. "You're faking Nicole, you can wipe away those false tears." "You never had true love for your child, but I did."

"That's not true, I love my baby girl and I want her to only have the best." "You could have fooled me!" "Here's what we're going to do!" "We're going to Nice, France in the morning and we're going to get her back and bring her home where she belongs!" Nicole sheepishly walked away whispering to herself. "No, we're not and you're never going to see her again." "After all, dead men don't talk."

CHAPTER 20

Sam woke up from his coma to two glaring eyes. Standing over the Governor was Mattie and Jake. He immediately panicked and grabbed for the buzzer to the nurse's station. Jake swiftly knocked it off the table. "No!" "We're not here to hurt you!" "Although I'd like to strangle you with my bare hands right now." "Especially for all the pain you've caused Mattie!" The Governor looked terrified. He looked to Mattie for any sign of sympathy, but she stood above him, looking down at Sam with hatred in her eyes.

"I don't feel sorry for you Sam." "You brought this all on yourself." Even though she knew that was a bold-faced lie. She felt empathy and pity for the man he had become. It wasn't in her nature to hold grudges and hatred, but the anger came naturally. "You set me up for Seth Jenkin's murder." "A murder you and Nicole Jenkins plotted together." The Governor looked surprised at Mattie's revelation.

"It took some time, but we pieced it together." "You're a murderer Sam." "You sent Antonio Scollini to my house!" "He shot my husband in the head!" "Ben had nothing to do with this!" "He just happened to be at the wrong place at the wrong time!" "Then you sent Nanny Rosa over to take my daughter and you sold her, sold her!" "You sold her to a couple in Switzerland so the police would think I had lost my mind out of guilt!"

She paused and took a deep long breath, shaking violently, finally exhaling slowly. "Then your dirty little secret came out." "Mr. Swartz found out who Melina really was didn't he?" "He planned on getting rid of my baby girl by tossing her over a bridge in a garbage bag!" "He was going to dump her like she was a piece of garbage!" Mattie was stoic and numb. She didn't like the anger that was encompassing her.

At this moment, she wondered what it would be like to slam a pillow on his face and watch him take his last breath. That thought scared her and brought her back to reality a little bit. Jake could sense she was stepping into a dark place. He pulled her away from Sam's bed. "Look at me!" "He can't hurt anyone ever, ever again!" "He's going to jail Mattie!" "This evil bastard is going to pay for his crimes!" "He's not going anywhere but a cold jail cell."

"Focus, look at me!" His eyes were locked directly on hers as if he could read her soul. "If you're still angry, fine!" "We'll deal with this together baby!" "Just remember why we're here!" "We don't have much time to find her!" "Can you do that?" She tightened her grip on his hands and smiled back at him. "You're right Jake!" She stared down at Sam, he looked sorrowful. He was pale and sickly looking. His hands were strapped to the bed. She had an epiphany.

Jake was right, he couldn't hurt anyone anymore. His plotting and scheming days were over. His hellish future was just getting started.

The thought that he finally would pay for all the hell he put her through gave her a sense of peace like she had never had before. The Governor spoke unexpectedly. "Mattie, I am so sorry for everything I've done." "You don't get to speak Sam, Jake countered. "No Jake let him speak." "This ought to be good, she thought. "I had my life planned out in Kentucky as the Governor for eight years." "I know Sam." "I was there planning your strategies and victories."

"I know you were there every step of the way." "When Seth Jenkins came along and started to steal my thunder, I got scared." "I felt like the people were turning on me." "Like they forgot all the great things I did for Kentucky." "Remember Mattie?" "Remember?" "Yes Sam, I remember." She said solemnly. "I guess I panicked." "I was such a fool."

"When Nicole Jenkins and I met it was like kindred spirits." She despised him almost as much as I did." "She wanted her freedom and I wanted the election more than anything." "She asked me to take care of her husband." "At first I was appalled by the idea." "I didn't want to do it, but she was quite the charmer." "She just wanted to be rid of him and I wanted him gone for good."

"Her only stipulation was that she couldn't be tied to anything." "So, I agreed to pay Scollini to get rid of our little problems." "I thought it would all go away."

"But then Nicole worried it could be traced back to her or me." "She said she had a new plan to take all the suspicion away from us." "I told her Scollini was a professional and he worked for me." "She would not listen!" "She said she sent pictures of her husband's murder to my office." "I flipped out and raced back to my office to get them because I knew you would be the first person to open all my mail." "Apparently so did Nicole." "I didn't know Mattie." "She went behind my back and did that."

"She also paid Scollini to ransack your house and shoot Ben." Mattie's heart dropped as she listened to every sick detail. "I tried to stop you from going home with those pictures." "I tried to stop it all, but it was too late." "So, I called Nanny Rosa and told her to go get Melina." "I was afraid Scollini would kill Melina too." "   He was a sick psychopath, he didn't care who he killed." "He just liked the game." "By the time you got home, I felt like I had no choice but to go along with Nicole as much as I hated it."

"I hated myself for doing it, but I wanted that election more than anything I ever wanted in my life." "I was empowered!" "I felt like a God that could change lives!"

Jake grabbed Mattie's hands. He was ready for her revenge on Governor Sam. She surprised him though. She nodded. Then she reached deep into her pockets, which almost jolted Sam out of the bed. She slowly pulled out a tape recorder and pushed stop. "Just thought I'd help the police out a little bit." Jake smiled, he was so proud of Mattie at this moment. "You didn't destroy my life Sam." "You wrecked it pretty good for awhile." "You destroyed yours." She glanced at Jake and smiled back.

"Now, the other reason I'm here." "I'm sure you already know Nicole has my other daughter stashed here somewhere in a boarding school." The Governor's eyes widened. "How did you know?" "When Jake and

I were investigating Nicole, we discovered she stole our newborn baby." "The nurse confessed." "We don't have much time Sam." "You want to make this right, don't you?"

Sam nodded and looked to her for his salvation. "Which boarding school is Nicolette in Sam?" He nodded, it was the least he could do for Mattie. "She's about ten miles up the road off of Napa Court." "The name of the school is La Petit." "What does our daughter look like Sam?" "She's short with dark hair." "She has Mattie's green eyes." "Good luck, God speed." Sam prayed that Mattie and Jake would get to La Petit before Nicole had the chance.

He knew his life would never be the same. The thought of spending his life in prison without daylight and fresh air and his freedom made him want to die. But he knew he deserved a lot worse. He was older now and had no fight left.

The sounds coming from the closet stirred him a bit. Someone stepped out of the closet just as he got his breath back. It was a nurse, how odd he thought. No, his eyes were playing tricks on him, he thought. It was his worst nightmare. She was smiling at him wickedly with her bright blue eyes. "Nicole, not again." "I'm already at death's door." "Did you come to finish me off?" He muttered impatiently.

"You're like a cat with nine lives Sam." "Today however, your number's up old friend." She turned and twisted dancing around his bed maliciously. "I can't believe you told Mattie and Jake how to get to my daughter." "You mean their daughter Nicole!" He whispered. He could sense this upset her and he liked the thought of having the last laugh and the last jab.

"Things are collapsing around you aren't they sweetheart?" "Oh, I'm not worried Sam." "They can't take her because they have no proof they're her real mommy and daddy." "Wanna bet?" "What do ya mean Sam?" "The nurse confessed and they have photos of you and Dr. McGowan." Nicole looked startled and her mouth was wide open. "How did they?" "How did they find out?" Sam retorted.

"They broke into Dr. McGowan's office obviously." He chuckled. "Your numbers up Nicole!" "It's time to pay for your sins as well." "You first Sam!" She took the pillow and slammed it on his face and suffocated him. Sam turned his face in the opposite direction, but he knew his time was up and it was useless. Sam was dead within minutes.

"Good night Sam, sweet dreams." Nicole exited immediately scouring left and right for witnesses. It was empty and quiet down the hall as she paced quickly cautiously waiting to the elevator. When she entered the elevator, she could hear the response to Sam's life support going off like bells and whistles. Several doctors and nurses were fleeing to Sam's room, but he was gone. The elevator doors closed as Nicole smiled brightly and uttered under her breath, "too late."

"Jake what if we don't get there in time?" "What if Nicole gets to her first?" "Don't worry we'll get there, baby." "And what if we can't take her home." "We'll get a lawyer." "Listen to me." "No judge in their right mind would continue to let Nicole have custody of that little girl." "We have all the proof we need!" "Go faster Jake, go faster!"

Meanwhile at the hospital, Nicole dispersed of the nurse's uniform in the garbage along with the white tights and white shoes. She couldn't wait to get them off. She couldn't understand why anyone would take a career that involved dressing conservatively every day. Never mind it was a respected occupation, saving lives and showing compassion to sick people.

She darted to the parking garage and took off like a bat out of hell in her silver Mercedes. She was worried about not getting to Nicolette in time, but she couldn't show Sam she was anxiety ridden and was afraid of losing control.

Nicole's first thought was of Nicolette. She just wanted to take her far, far away where no one could get to her or tell her the truth about whose daughter she really was. She called Nicolette at La Petit frantic to speak with her. The phone rang several times as Nicole's heart jetted. Her heart skipped a few beats taking her breath away. Finally, after the fifth ring, Nicolette answered. "Hi, Mommy!" "Nicolette, sweetheart, where were you?" "Never mind, she snapped.

"I'm coming to get you and take you out of that school forever!" "Wouldn't you like that?" Nicolette laughed jubilantly. "But mommy, I'm not there anymore." "What!" Nicole screamed. "Where are you?" "Who are you with?"

"Mattie and Jake, she uttered under her breath. Nicolette was having a conversation with someone in the background. Nicole could hear his voice, it almost seemed familiar. Strangely familiar. "Can I tell her yet?" Nicole was terrified, on the edge of her seat. "Nicolette quit playing games and tell me who you're with right now!" She demanded. "That's funny, Grandpa said you love playing games." Nicole's heart stopped. She couldn't breathe, she was in dire straits.

She knew Nicolette had no grandparents. Her parents died when she was in high school and Seth's parents died when he was a teenager as well. "Give me the phone honey!" "Nicole, pull over right now before you wreck!" "Nicolette is fine!" "You however, a completely different story!" She knew that voice. It was strong, masculine, and very authoritative.

She heard it thousands of times. "Pull over now, so we can talk." "Please Nicole." Nicole pulled over to the side of the road. It was just a few miles from La Petit. She finally caught a breath. "I thought you were dead." "Daaaaaaaaaaaad!" "Bernard Wayne Sutton has risen from the grave!" "How did you escape?" "The car went over the ridge." "Yes, Nicole it did." "Your mother was driving when we went over that ridge." "When we crashed it killed her instantly."

"There was nothing I could do for her." "I pulled myself out of the car to get help, but I didn't want to leave her in there. "I went back to get her and the car exploded into a fireball." "Why didn't you tell someone?" "Why didn't you come back for me?" She pressed him on this hard. "After all these years you made me think you were dead!" She snarled. "Why would you do such a cruel thing to me?"

There was dead silence for a moment. "I'm sorry Nicole." He paused and took a deep, deep breath. "I just wanted to be free from responsibilities." "I'm really sorry honey." "Where have you been all these years?" "Somewhere where I could keep an eye on my two daughters growing up." "I was never that far away." "Why would you leave me, she demanded. "I needed you!"

You were never there for me and mom!" "Your heart and mind were never there!" He sighed heavily. "I don't know what to tell you Nicole." "You were always so demanding of my attention." "Even when I was right there with you, it was never enough. "I just needed to be free to the things I needed to do." "Nicole are you there?" "I'm here." "Why you know what, that's fine." "I got by on my own just fine without you." "I never needed anyone."

"People just get in the way of your plans." "Like Nicolette!" "I love my little girl!" "I love her!" "She knows that!" "You mean Mattie's little girl!" "What!" "No, no Dad she's mine!" "Nicolette belongs to Mattie, your sister!" "How stupid do you think I am?" "Doesn't matter." "How did you know?" "It doesn't matter Nicole." "I'm setting things right." "Give me back my daughter!" She pleaded. "I took her so I could raise your grandchild."

"Mattie never wanted her anyway." She rationalized. "She was going off to school and leaving Beaver Dam." "It doesn't matter Nicole, she wasn't yours to take." "What about Nicolette?" "Don't worry, she's watching a movie in the back." "She doesn't know what's going on yet." "I'm the only mother she's ever known." Nicole pleaded with him. "Please Dad, give me back my little girl!" She was sobbing uncontrollably.

"Nicolette, talk to your mother, she misses you very much!" "Hi little girl, I miss you very much." She could barely could get the words out. "I love you, sweet little girl!" "There, there now." "You talked to her, she's fine." "Where are you taking Nicolette?" "Remember the run for the roses?" "Floppy hats, mint juleps!" "Why we're going to Churchill Downs of course!"

"We'll have our own father-daughter reunion and you can say goodbye to Nicolette!" "Then I'm giving her back to Mattie and Jake!" He said matter of fact. "You're taking my daughter back to Kentucky!" She said astonished. "Noooooooo!" She shouted into the phone. "I'll see you there tonight at 7 pm." "Please, no, you can't do that to me!" It was too late, Nicole knew there was no pleading or bargaining with her father.

She called the airline and took the next flight back to Louisville, Kentucky. Mattie and Jake got the shocking news from the head master at La Petit. Their daughter was long gone and had left with a man calling himself Grandpa. Mattie was livid and wanted answers immediately. The head master explained to them that Nicole had sent him to get her and they would be returning to Kentucky.

He also left a note for Mattie and Jake where they could retrieve their little girl. Mattie and Jake were astounded. "Nicole's got her!" "How did she know we were coming to get Nicolette?" "I might have an idea about that, Jake responded.

He called the hospital to check on Sam and received the bad news. Then he called Lt. Thacker for the whole story. "He died this morning." 'We're still investigating what happened." "We found a nurse's outfit in the trash outside." "We also have surveillance of an unidentified woman walking out of the building. "Nicole!" "Yes, that would be our first guess." "She has our daughter!" Jake was furious. "I can't believe you let her go!" "She's a murderer!"

"Don't worry, we'll find her!" "We'll get your little girl back!" "Don't bother!" "She's going to be on our turf now!" "Hello, Jake slammed the phone down. "Nicole was in Sam's room while we were there!" "That's the only way she could have known we were on our way to La Petit." "Read the note Jake, maybe it'll tell us where she is."

They looked at each other for signs of hope, but they knew. Nicole always seemed to be one step ahead of them. She was smart about planning ahead. They were afraid for their daughter and her well-being.

Mattie and Jake: I know you must be very worried about your daughter. No worries, she's fine. She's with her grandfather. Just know that she is safe and happy. I had to get her out of there before Nicole could get to her. Before you waste any more time looking for her, we are on our way back to Kentucky. I will bring your daughter to Churchill Downs. I have already purchased two tickets for you both. Go to the airport now. You should just be able to make the next flight.

Please do not bring the police into this. Let's just keep this simple. I look forward to seeing my two daughters tonight together. I know you have a lot of questions, I will answer them all.

Sincerely,
Bernard Wayne Sutton

"Oh my God Jake!" "Bernard Wayne Sutton is my real dad!" "He's supposed to be dead!" "He's the one your mother had the affair with?" "Yeah, I guess so!" Mattie and Jake were bewildered about what to do first. "I'll call Lil'J and tell him what's going on." "No!" "Mattie, listen to me!" "We're going to need some backup, he and his men can stay in the background." Mattie agreed. "Let's just get to the airport and get on that plane to Louisville before it's too late!" Jake called Lil'J but he was out the whole day. The lieutenant said he was taking a personal day. Jake left a message anyway. He hoped it would reach him in time. He didn't want the entire KSP showing up. He wanted things quiet and safe, just until they could get to the bottom of things. Jake just wanted to know what was really going on.

As Mattie lay sleeping in Jake's arms, a message appeared on her phone from Bernard Wayne. There will be a limousine waiting for you both outside the airport. He reminded them to keep the silence. No police. I know you both have questions and I want to answer them all. I also look forward to making things right. Tonight, many wrongs will be undone and you can finally plan a future together with Nicolette. Nicole will pay for her crimes against you both.

Jake was taken aback. He didn't know if this was a trustworthy man or if he was just telling them what they wanted to hear. Nicole received a text from her Dad as well. She was furious at her father for screwing up all her plans. She had no intentions of coming back to Kentucky. But she refused to give up Nicolette to Mattie and Jake.

Meanwhile at Churchill Downs, it was ten o' clock. Bernard Wayne waited patiently for the arrival of his first daughter Nicole to pull up in the limousine. He loved everything about Churchill Downs. He'd been to almost every derby. He loved the excitement of it all. He loved the ladies in their floppy hats, dressed to the nines, accessorizing with their long slinky white gloves, and sipping mint juleps.

He loved the light and cheerful conversations and the great anticipation of the final race.

Churchill Downs was surrounded by much history of the greatest horse races and the jockeys whose claim to fame by their first big win. But Bernard wasn't thinking about history tonight. Tonight, he was focused on the present moment and how it would affect everyone's future. He smiled at Nicolette who was eagerly awaiting Nicole as well. As the limousine pulled up to the track, Bernard and Nicolette took a deep breath. Nicole stepped out of the limousine slowly.

She looked haggard and beaten. Her heart was racing. She didn't know what to expect. Her beautiful, long blonde hair was pulled back in a ponytail. She was dressed very conservatively. Her black suit draped her body magnificently. Tonight, she wasn't the skilled seductress or the deceitful schemer. Tonight, she was for the moment, a mother who loved her little girl.

She was daddy's little girl. Nicole loved her father very much. She could never understand why he would leave her and betray her by giving her daughter back to Mattie. Nicole stood still for a moment, wrangling her hands. She adjusted her suit and collected her thoughts. She hoped and prayed God would forgive her for what she was about to do. Bernard was anxiety ridden as well.

As he stood looking at his beautiful daughter, all he could see was a monster and a murderer. He couldn't understand why his love and attention were never enough for her. He was truly frightened of her and hoped things would go well. Nicole smiled sheepishly at Nicolette and walked slowly toward them.

She stopped a few feet away and slowly dropped to her knees and held out her arms to Nicolette. Nicolette was hesitant at first and looked toward her grandfather. Nicolette broke free of his grip and ran to Nicole. He knew Nicole needed this closure, so he stood over her cautiously waiting for his daughter to make a scene or run away with her. "I missed you so much Nicolette!" Out of nowhere Nicolette slapped her and knocked her to the ground. "I know what you did Nicole!"

"I know what you did to Seth and you're not my mother!" She spat in her face and ran back to Bernard. Nicole was devastated. Tears streamed down her face. Her little girl was hers no more. She was theirs. This was the last straw. Nicole looked like a puma ready to pounce. Bernard could see she was agitated and angry. He stood tall and ordered Nicolette into the limousine until things calmed down.

"Nicolette, stop!" "Don't listen to him!" "He's lying to you!" "You turned my daughter against me!" "How dare you!" "I'm not your little girl, my mommies name is Mattie and my daddy's name is Jake!" "No, no, no!" Nicole was desperate to fix this. "Ok Nicolette!" "It's true, I took you from Mattie, because she didn't want you and I did.

"So, I took her place instead and I raised you and loved you!" "Just as you were my own!"

Nicolette go to the car and wait for me!" "It's not safe!" Nicolette did as she was told to do and raced to the car jumping in head first. She was scared too. "You bastard!" "You turned her against me!" He knew things were about to spiral out of control. All he could do now was calm things down. "Nicole, I would never hurt you in a million years." "You're my daughter!" "I love you!" She deserved the truth. "All I want to do now is get you the help that you need."

"I promise I'll never leave you again!" "You're my baby." "I want to take care of you now." "Do you believe me?" Nicole looked spent and worn down. She flashed him a half-hearted grin. He extended his hand towards her and she slowly walked towards him. They embraced and held each other for a minute. "It's all going to be ok Nicole, he was deftly interrupted by a sharp pain in his chest.

Nicole's blaring hatred for her father represented itself with a six-inch kitchen knife she secretly hid in her sleeve. Bernard dropped to the ground writhing in pain. Bernard knew Nicole's intent. But he was surprised by her reaction. He realized there was no reasoning with her and started sliding back on the ground. Nicole had turned the tables on him. "You think you've won!" "Then you don't know me too well Dad!" "Nicolette is mine!" "You don't get to finish this!" She screamed for the world to hear. "Please Nicole, don't do this to your daughter!" He held out his hands pleading for her to stop, but he knew it was too late.

He was going to die here and poor Nicolette would be trapped with a psychopathic mother who would stop at nothing to get her way. As she stepped over him with the shiny sharp-edged blade, he screamed in terror. She maliciously raised the knife for the final kill. She was unaware of a dark tall shadow behind her. Jake grabbed Nicole by the neck and flung her to the ground like a sumo wrestler. He grabbed the knife and tossed it aside. She was completely taken by surprise.

Armageddon descended upon Churchill Downs. Lil'J received Jake's message later that afternoon. The Kentucky State Police, Swat teams and the F.B.I. appeared around every corner. Nicole was on the F.B.I.'s most wanted list and they were going to have their heyday.

Nicole was taken away in handcuffs screaming at the top of her lungs. "You haven't heard the last from me!" "I will have my revenge on all of you!" "Lil'J to the rescue!" Lil'J approached Mattie and Jake with a big smile. "I told you guys I'd be there for you." Mattie and Jake gave Lil'J a big hug and thanked him. Bernard was in a lot of pain, but wanted so desperately to speak with his daughter. Mattie stared at him with disbelief. "Wait!" "I need to speak to Mattie before you take me away!"

"Where's Nicolette!" "Don't worry Mattie, she's safe in the limousine." "She's being watched by one of my officers."

She breathed a heavy sigh of relief. "Bernard you're hurt." "Don't worry about me Mattie, I'll be fine." She could tell he was in a lot of pain and right now wasn't the time for all the answers she wanted so badly. She grabbed his hand and kissed his cheek. "Thank you for bringing me back my daughter Bernard." "You're my hero." "Mattie, go be with your daughter."

"She needs you and Jake now." As the ambulance took him away, she wondered what was to become of him. Would she ever truly know just how much he sacrificed for her tonight. She looked at Lil'J and Jake with a heavy heart. "Mattie, he'll be fine." They reassured her. "I believe there's a little girl waiting for both of you." "She wants her mommy and daddy." "Ya gonna keep her waiting?" He smiled.

Mattie and Jake looked at each other lovingly. Jake put his arm around Mattie. "It's been a hell of a day." She nodded. "Let's go meet our little girl Mattie." "I'm ready whenever you are." They walked hurriedly to the long black limousine. In an instant, their life was going to change forever. Lil'J bellowed for his waiting officer to open the door. The only thing they could hear was the crickets chirping.

It felt like sunshine stepping out of the door for Mattie and Jake. Their hearts dropped and mouths were wide open. Nicolette looked like her daddy. She had long brown hair and big green eyes like Mattie.

She wore a pink ribbon in her hair and a pink ruffled dress and a smile as big as the Derby.

She ran to them instantly and they held on to each other for a long time. Finally, they were together, they were a family. They were reunited and ready to start their new life together. Mattie and Jake cried uncontrollably as they held their daughter. But she surprised them both. She laughed and giggled and warmed their hearts. They were ready to start a new future together and let go of the intrepid past that almost swallowed them whole.

Six months later, Nicole was declared too insane to stand trial for the murders of Seth Jenkins and Governor Sam Waters. She was sent to the sanitarium in Lexington. She was sentenced to two life sentences. The doctor's prognosis was schizophrenia. She was heavily sedated most of the time and she kept to herself. The doctors were happy with her prognosis with each meeting. They believed she was under their control. Nicole however, had other plans.

Mattie and Jake were married six months later in Lexington. It was a beautiful small ceremony surrounded by their families and friends and two beloved daughters. Nicolette demanded to have her name changed to Eva Catherine. Jake went to the police academy in Richmond, Kentucky and passed with flying colors. He became a police officer and Mattie continued to work with domestically abused women which was her passion in life.

Mattie had just put the girls to bed eagerly waiting for Jake to come home. Everything was normal and routine. She finally felt safe again with Jake. He was her stronghold. All the craziness of the past seemed to dissipate in the air. She could breathe again. She felt grounded and happy, like nothing could touch their family. There was a violent thunderstorm blaring in Lexington that night. Normally, this would have scared her, but nothing phased her now. She wasn't scared anymore. She was strong and fearless and so happy with her life and Jake and the girls.

The storm was brutal. Sixty miles per hour trade winds blowing everything out of sight. The electricity went off. The house went black. Mattie wasn't scared though, not yet. She was just very annoyed. She hopped from each room lighting candles until she could find her way to the basement door to the generator.

She cautiously opened the door. It was dark, but it had to be done. She put on her brave face and tip-toed slowly down the creaky wooden stairs with a flashlight in her hand. It was creepy. It reminded her of a bad scene from a horror movie. Again, she laughed. She had to remind herself she was ferocious and fearless. As she made her way to the generator box, she looked around the room. Checking everything in sight. She stopped for a moment, reliving all the wonderful memories surrounding her. She noticed a box with Melina's plush white teddy bear and a photo album with her wedding pictures in it.

This put a big smile on her face. She felt silly for being so creeped out by the basement. "I'm an idiot, if Jake were here, he would laugh." She whispered to herself. She found the generator box breathing a sigh of relief. Not for long, however. The hairs on the back of her neck stood up. She wasn't alone. She flipped around to scream at Jake for scaring her, but it wasn't Jake. Instead, she was met with a sharp hypodermic needle tearing at the nape of her neck.

She fell to the floor immediately, numb. She was paralyzed from whatever lethal drug that was injected into her. She couldn't move at all. Not her fingers, her toes, her hands. She laid on the cold, stone floor lifeless. She began falling in and out of consciousness. The room was hazy. Her breathing became slow and shallow. She tried to move. It was useless.

A tall, blonde woman was kneeling over her. Her icy blue eyes were lit up with excitement and anticipation. "You took everything from me!" "Now I'm going to take what's mine." She flashed her a fake sympathetic smile. "Good night Mattie."

The End

Made in the USA
Columbia, SC
03 December 2017